# Self Made

## M. Darusha Wehm

Self Made
by M. Darusha Wehm

Published by *in potentia press*

Copyright 2010 M. Darusha Wehm

ISBN 978-0-9737467-3-0

http://darusha.ca/selfmade

## Books by M. Darusha Wehm

*Beautiful Red*

*Children of Arkadia*

Andersson Dexter novels:

*Self Made*

*Act of Will*

*The Beauty of Our Weapons*

# ONE

THE MOMENT SHE walked into the joint, Dex had known that she was there for him. It wasn't just the hard look about her, the one that says, "I've never been in a dive like this before but I'll be damned if I'm going to let the creeps and low lifes scare me". It wasn't even the fact that she stuck out like a naked face. Really, he knew because she walked in. Everyone else would have ported in from a link, but she didn't have a link. And that meant she'd been looking for this place on the QT and that meant she'd been looking for him.

That was the previous day. The memory of the meeting was fresh but imperfect, so Dex paged over to his viewer. His hands tripped across the space in front of him, moving files and links out of his view. The space he was sitting in was close, but there was enough room for him to easily wave his arms around — he could have expanded his viewer's size to maybe even double without having to worry about whacking his neighbour. He found the file he wanted and the video image of his meeting the previous day imposed itself over his vision.

Dex, like most people, used one eye for one task, the other eye for another one, with the whole mess at about 80% opacity so he could still just see the physical world in front of him. At work he didn't really need to see at all, but you never can be too careful. Just because he kept his own screen at a reasonable size didn't mean that someone nearby, playing with the resolution, wouldn't inadvertently punch him in the head while just trying to delete some mail.

He flicked a finger to start running the file, but then a chime sounded. Fuck. A call. He'd have to answer it, since that was how he kept his job and got paid. He quickly flicked his fingers in front of him, simultaneously hiding the file, opening a program on the company's system and answering the call. "Barrett and Brar Upgrades, how may I help you make a better you?"

Dex gave the required greeting, then listened as the customer explained how his new neural sensation enhancer was malfunctioning. Dex had to suppress a chuckle as the guy at the other end of the call's voice quivered as he spoke. Dex ran through the troubleshooting procedures with the caller, but early on down the litany of questions about configuration and whether the customer actually had turned the unit on, his mind wandered back to the meeting with the new client. And his real job.

• • •

Andersson Dexter had been working for Barrett and Brar for going on ten years now, but he'd been working for The Cubicle Men most of his life. He'd taken a series of fairly dull jobs over the course of his adult life, usually as a Customer Service Rep, just like most of the other Cubicle Men did. Being a Cubicle Man wasn't a job; it was a vocation.

He had been working for a low end laser keyboard manufacturer, back before the touch screens everyone used now had become common, when he first learned of the organization. He'd been walking home one night after an extra long long shift, when he heard a sound from around a corner. In the previous few months, the local boards had been reporting that there had been a rash of street violence and Dex figured he'd stumbled upon some local hoods trying to stake their claim to this patch of concrete. Dex's eyes flicked to the corner, where the sounds of scuffling and a few loud bangs and whimpers drew his attention. He tried to ignore the sounds and kept walking toward his apartment.

He got closer and the sounds got worse. Dex thought he heard something breaking and crossed the street. He could see down the alley and saw a couple of young guys beating on a pair of streeters. The victims weren't even fighting back; they almost looked like inert piles of rags, as the young toughs kicked, punched and spat at them. Dex slunk back against the wall of the building behind him, trying to disappear into the shadows, when he saw a couple of other people arrive on the scene and break up the fight. At first he assumed it was younger or stronger streeters coming to the aid of their compatriots, but then he saw they were all dressed in what looked like Security uniforms. But they weren't Security from any firm Dex could identify and he was familiar with all the local outfits.

Dex kept to the shadows, half hidden behind a light standard and watched. The men pulled the attackers away and restrained them. Then one of their number methodically socked each one of the attackers in the gut. He must have had some kind of weapon, a stunner or knuckledusters, because each one of the attackers he hit fell like a stone. By the time the muscle man got to the last guy, he didn't even really need to hit him, the guy was so scared. But hit him he did and the young would-be tough joined his pals face down in the gutter, clutching his gut. Dex waited until these new guys split and when he was sure he wouldn't be seen, Dex hurried back to his room. Once he was safe inside and munching on a nutrient bar, he pulled up the recording he'd made of the incident.

Since before he'd even gotten his first real job, Dex had spent most of his disposable income on disk upgrades, both locally stored and online backups. Most people recorded their lives to some extent, at least a couple of minutes on delay so they could always save an important or special moment. But Dex wanted it all. He would never be able to afford enough disk to keep it all, but as a rule he deleted only the most mundane of daily moments, so he was easily able to call up the video of these strange men.

He spent most of the night working with the video. He processed it and uploaded it to the public cross referencing engines on the 'nets, looking for any information about the men who beat up the local hoods. He didn't get very far — the resolution was pretty bad since they were a good distance away and Dex's default resolution was fairly low to begin with — anything to get more on the disk. He eventually gave up and after a few weeks even stopped looking. He hadn't forgotten, he just stopped caring. It was too much work for something that was just a passing curiosity to begin with. Then he got the message.

He was at work, asking another idiot customer if the keyboard was connected to a power source, when his messenger tinkled. Dex liked auditory notification, so under the sounds of the customer's curses he heard the sound of windchimes as the message was received. He brought up the message, which was text only. Dex scanned the message and whispered aloud, "What the fuck." The customer he was helping stopped his rambling and asked, "Did you say something?"

"No, sorry," Dex recovered, "Just some background noise here. You were saying..." The customer kept on with his tale of mismatched cabling while Dex re-read the message.

"Andersson Dexter," the message began.

"You have been looking for us. After analyzing your profile, we have determined that you do not seem to be interested in our services as a client. Therefore we must conclude that you are interested in our operations for other reasons.

"We invite you to meet a representative at the linked location at 1500 UTC tomorrow. We will meet you there."

The message was unsigned and the return address was a popular anonymizer service. But Dex knew it was the men he had seen handing out some kind of street justice. And they wanted to meet him.

• • •

The link in the message was for a location online that Dex was unfamiliar with, but it was in one of the normal zones. He was confident that he could link into the location and he'd be able to maneuver his avatar without having to deal with altered laws of physics or anything out of the ordinary. But he was still unsure. Dex spent the next day debating with himself about what he should do. First thing in the morning, he'd decided to ignore the message. He didn't need the hassle. By the time he was on the train on the way to work, though, Dex wasn't so sure. He couldn't stop wondering what would happen if he kept the date. Once he'd arrived at his work station he knew that there wasn't really any question any more. If he let it go, he knew that he'd spend the rest of his life wondering what might have happened and he had enough regrets already.

When the time came, Dex followed the link in the message. He found his virtual self in a large open building that reminded him of the time he'd been in the back of an upgrade salon, only without all the stuff. There wasn't even a bench to sit his virtual self upon while he waited. Dex couldn't see any other avatar there and after he'd wandered around and determined that he really was alone, two more avatars linked in. There was one female and one androgynous looking creature and they walked toward him. "Andersson Dexter," the female-looking avatar said, the voice a decent machine-replicated tone.

"Yes," he said, one part of his mind prepared to back out of the simulation at the first sign of trouble. A weapon, for example. But these people gave no sign of violence. Seeming to read his thoughts, the one who had first spoken to him said, "Don't worry. There's no need to fear. We are unarmed." After all, Dex had done nothing wrong and as it turned out, these people were only interested in those people who were wrongdoers.

The androgynous one explained that since law enforcement, if you could even call it that, was practically left to the Security departments of the firms, they only protected their own employees and only to the extent that it benefitted the firm. There were plenty of people who were essentially alone in the world and some crimes that would always go unpunished because the victim was unemployed or the crime didn't actually inconvenience the employers in any way. It was a complicated problem, the avatar explained, but the solution wasn't complicated at all.

They were part vigilante, part private detective and part cop. The organization operated as a check and balance on its members, ensuring that the individual members didn't go off half cocked. They had rules, procedures, even shifts. But they operated under the radar, independent of any firm. Their members all had other jobs to ensure they had access to housing and healthcare, but they were expected to work at low level jobs — their real work was being cops where there was otherwise only anarchy.

It was a rousing speech and Dex was impressed. He could tell that he was getting recruited and it didn't bother him. It didn't really excite him, either, but they had let slip that there was under the table pay and there were some clear side benefits. The organization had access to some pretty cutting edge personal electronics and he would get to do something more interesting with his mind than ask consumer grade morons if they'd tried turning it off and on.

Of course, he signed up.

• • •

That had been twenty years previously and Dex had risen through the ranks fairly quickly. He discovered early on that he truly liked the work and demonstrated a definite aptitude for it. He first expected that he'd make a pretty good goon, but as it happened he was actually more inclined to sort out puzzles than sap guys on the head, so now found himself as a Lieutenant in the detective squad. The organization took its structure from historical police departments, though functionally once people advanced out of the goon squad, they operated more or less independently.

The organization was really a loose group of individuals who pooled resources and shared information. It didn't even have an official name. One of the detectives who had worked in Dex's division years before was a fan of old superhero comics, though, and for laughs started calling the squad the Cubicle Men — nondescript people who work at faceless jobs in cubicles by day and fight crime by night, that sort of thing. The name stuck and soon spread throughout the Namerican branch of the organization and by the time Dex joined everyone in his zone referred to themselves by the lighthearted name.

The captains of each detective squad often assigned cases, though each member of the team was free to refuse a case or ask to work on a particular file. Or a particular detective would get a reputation and clients would just show up. Dex's meeting the previous day was one of those, but he would have asked to work on this one anyway, if it had come up for grabs. The case was fairly unusual, after all, and Dex did enjoy the strange and unusual. He looked at the still image of his client while explaining to the customer on the call how to calibrate the new neural enhancers. Her avatar was pleasing to his eye, he had to admit, but that wasn't why Dex was staring. It just wasn't every day that you got to investigate the murder of your client.

# TWO

DEX FINALLY FINISHED his service call and after completing the millions of required forms for B&B, he opened the video record of his conversation with the client. They had met online in the seedy bar that Dex was known to frequent. Three Card Monte's Bar, a common spot for Cubicle Men to get together and talk shop, was off the map. Literally. There was a public map of Marionette City, much like a directory or an index. Of course, the vast majority of places an avatar could go were not on the map — you could search for them if you knew what you were looking for, but mostly it was word of mouth. A friend of a friend gave you a link, or someone on a board posted directions.

It was obviously by following directions that she had found the place. Her avatar was wary as she entered the bar, but she showed no sign of turning back. He hadn't seen it at the time, but watching the video Dex figured she was one of those people who was fully aware of the reality that the interface was a simulation. The realistic feel of the three-dimensional virtual reality interface to the everywherenet, popularly known as Marionette City, was both the reason for its popularity and also its major flaw. People often forgot that the rules were a little different there.

But she seemed to be holding her own. She walked into the place and after scanning the crowd, made a bee-line for Dex. Her avatar was probably patterned after her physical world looks, since it was a popular female body shape that season, with green hair falling just past the bottom of her ears. Since it was almost as easy to change the shape of physical bodies as it was to change an avatar, many people matched their real world and online looks. The avatar's face was pretty, in the pale shade that was currently fashionable and had a number of silver studs dotting its surface. On a physical face they would be the implants conferring some kind of upgrade to the built in computer system everyone wore inside their heads. Dex's own face was covered, almost all of them disk upgrades.

But she looked fairly average, as she walked toward Dex, green hair sparkling in the false light. She stopped at his table, opened her mouth to start to say something then stopped. "You lost?" Dex asked.

"I don't think so, Mr. Dexter," she answered.

He smiled without warmth and asked, "You're in trouble, then?"

The female avatar frowned slightly, then said, "I have a... situation. I was told that I could get it solved here."

"You got a job?" Dex asked, bluntly, his avatar sipping a short rum and ginger beer from a cut glass tumbler while his physical body was slurping dishwater coffee from a B&B mug.

"Yes," she said, "but this doesn't have to do with that."

"Still," Dex said, putting the drink on the table, "cops are usually one of the benefits of employment. You can't just go to your Security for this... situation?"

She sighed and her avatar started to look a little angry. Watching the video Dex could see the signs of a user who was quite familiar with the technology at work in rendering an avatar in Marionette City. Her avatar had complex facial expressions that were not part of the default package. Maybe she was a programmer or a UI designer. He didn't ask, because she made it clear that talking about her job was something she wasn't planning to do a lot of and it didn't matter to Dex anyway.

"Look," she said, planting her hands on the table and leaning over it toward Dex. "This is not the kind of situation I can take to Security. Not only would they not help me, I could maybe even get fired for it. So, no. I can't go to Security." She leaned back and seemed to take a deep breath. "Can you help me," she asked, "or am I wasting both of our time here?"

Dex picked up his empty glass and watched as it filled itself. He took a sip and gestured with the glass to the other chair at the table.

"Have a seat."

• • •

She said her name was Ivy Velasquez and Dex wasn't sure whether that was her real name or a name she invented for his benefit. It didn't really matter; the funds she transferred to the organization's escrow account were real enough. She sat at the table in silence for a moment and Dex just let her sit. He had found over the years that getting people to talk was as easy as creating a void for them to fill. It worked for irate customers who swore at you, too. It was amazing how powerful shutting up for a moment could be.

As usual, the silence finally got to her and she started to explain. "It happened about a week ago. I was at home, it was my weekend. I went to log in to Marionette City and I couldn't. I wasn't getting errors or lag, it was as if the login process was wrong somehow. I checked everything to make sure I was using the right schematic..."

Dex stopped her. "What do you mean, the right schematic? You just log in automatically — it's the same authentication no matter how you get into the 'nets — hell, there shouldn't be a login sequence at all."

"Yeah," Ivy sighed. "I know. But," she looked around, even though they were talking on a private channel, "I was logging in as a multi. I have another identity. Well... had, I guess."

Dex took a sip of his drink and sat back. "Okay," he said. "That explains a lot."

Even though Dex didn't say anything else, she was already on the defensive. "There's nothing wrong with it, you know," Ivy said, her voice taking on a strident quality. "Sometimes people just change, or want to try something new, it's no big deal." Her hands made a smoothing motion over her iridescent white dress that looked like a nervous habit. Watching the video, Dex paused and reran the sequence. He wondered, not for the first time, if Ivy's avatar was hooked directly into her physical responses. It was fairly trivial to do and made for a much more realistic experience. It just wasn't that common, since it was an undocumented feature of the three-dimensional interface. And it made Ivy's avatar look like she was lying, like she had something to hide. Not the smartest move, Dex thought.

"Okay, it's no big deal," he said, holding her gaze. "But I know that most employers have a no multis clause in their contracts – they don't want other identities sneaking around on company property, so to speak. So, I can see why you wouldn't want to go to Security with this." Dex swirled the ice cubes in his drink then put it on the table. "What makes you think this is a problem for me," he asked. "I'm not a programmer — I can't debug your system."

Ivy's avatar's eyes closed and opened again slowly. "I don't need a programmer," she said. "It wasn't user error. When I couldn't get in, I logged in as..." She looked a bit sheepish as she gestured at her avatar body, "this and I..." Her voice choked slightly. She regained her composure and finished, "I found the... ah... the body."

"Really?" He knew his response was not as compassionate as it could have been, but Dex was curious. "There were remains?"

"Yes," Ivy said, sounding a bit surprised that Dex would ask. "I finally figured out that reason I couldn't log in was that Reuben — that's Reuben Cobalt, my multi — was already logged in. I pinged him and tracked him down to an empty area not far from here." The bar was in a less developed part of the topography of Marionette City, the better to avoid unnecessary walk-in traffic. "I found him there... it was..." Her voice choked again and Dex waited for her to get herself together. "It was horrible."

She started to describe what she found, but eventually gave up and just sent Dex an image of the scene. He paged away from the video and brought up the high res image. He had to give her credit, she'd had the presence of mind to capture the image before leaving the scene. The image showed an avatar, or what was left of one, lying prone and limp — it reminded Dex more of a deflated sex doll than a human corpse. Even so, Dex could tell that the avatar would have been striking — a tall, thin, male form, with almost silver hair short against his scalp. In this state the hair looked a bit like dull wire, but Dex guessed that it would have shone with luminescence when animated.

But it wasn't just the lack of movement or "life" that made it clear that the avatar was fundamentally broken. It was the cuts. Dex didn't know what else to call them. It wasn't just the clothes, it was the whole form of the avatar's body that looked like it had been ripped apart. Dex magnified the image and could see lines of code at the edge of the tears, as if the very essence of the avatar had been destroyed. He paged back to the video and skipped ahead to Ivy's explanation of what she'd found after taking the remains offline.

"He was recoded," she said, obviously fighting to keep the emotion from her voice now. "Whoever did this broke into the coding of the avatar, wiped the memory and recoded him. They put him into a loop and I..." Her voice cracked. "He tore himself apart." She put her head in her hands and her avatar's body shook slightly. Dex put a hand on her shoulder and she jumped at his touch. "I'm sorry," she said, "I'm just not ready..."

"It's fine," Dex said, pulling his hand away and reaching for his drink. He silently finished it off and when it was done he didn't refill the glass. "We'll need to talk more about this," he finally said to her. "Here's a direct link to this place and my messenger address." He sent her the links and stood up. "I know they wiped the memory, but I'll need anything you have left from Reuben. Did you ever communicate between, ah, this identity and that one?"

"No," she said. "I was... I wanted to leave this one behind." She looked at Dex and he thought he could see tears in the avatar's eyes. "I hardly even answer to Ivy anymore. In my heart... when I think of myself... it's Reuben."

The video ended. Dex had left her there when he linked out of the bar. There was no point in him hanging around; there wasn't anything he could do for her there. Besides, that place had seen its share of people alone, crying into their virtual drinks.

• • •

When Dex's shift at B&B ended, he left the building and walked the block or so to the train stop. He used the time to check some messages and sign in to the organization's network. His messenger popped up a text alert reminding him that his stock of nutrient bricks was getting dangerously low, so he got off the train a stop early and headed into the neighbourhood grocery. He picked up a bulk carton of Econoline, the cheapest brand on sale and as he walked to the door, his eye fell on the booze display.

His messenger hadn't alerted him to a drop in the rum supply, but Dex had never gotten around to recalibrating the notification to his particular specifications. He didn't want to have to worry, so he picked up a litre bottle of Jamaica's Best. It was synthesized in a factory near Shanghai and wasn't even in the top ten out of that shop, but it got the job done. As he walked out the door, an alert flashed in his vision noting the charge for the provisions and informing him that his account had been debited accordingly. He walked the couple of blocks to his apartment and shouldered his way through the beaten steel door. His room was on the 48th floor and he stepped into the lift to let the spiral carry him up to his floor. After about half a minute he stepped off at his floor and after a few steps down the concrete and steel hall he heard the lock of his door responding to the chip embedded under the skin of his hand.

The door shushed open and Dex stepped in. The room was small, but he didn't need a lot. He stowed the fresh box of Econoline bricks on the floor below the water tap and zapper. He shook the last few bricks out of the previous box, opening one and taking a bite of the chewy, brown mass. He stuffed the old box in the recyclatron and left the remaining bars on top of the new box. He put the new bottle of Jamaica's Best into the cupboard, taking out the open, quarter full bottle and a tumbler. With the food brick wedged in his teeth, Dex opened the rum and poured a generous portion into the tumbler. He opened the cooler and pulled out a can of Gingapop. It wasn't as good as real ginger beer, but that was expensive and hard to come by, so Dex made do. He popped open the can and splashed a bit of the soda into the glass and stirred it with his index finger. He took a long drink, then sat at his small table.

Before he forgot, Dex paged over to the Cubicle Men's system and logged the time he'd spent reviewing the record of his meeting with Ivy. He wasn't paid by the hour and it really didn't matter, but the organization liked to keep track of the both the time each member spent on a case, but also how much of their regular job time they were using for the organization's work. They didn't just fill a niche that the firms left blank; the Cubicle Men were philosophically opposed to the prevailing social system, so they encouraged their members to use their employer's time and resources as much as possible. Getting caught and subsequently fired would be going too far, though. It would certainly be possible to survive without a mainstream job, but it would be unnecessarily difficult.

Dex read over a few internal memos, logged his time and paged out of the system. He knew that he ought to review the information about the Ivy/Reuben case, but he just didn't feel like it. He didn't have any information other than what was on the video and the image and he'd gone over that at B&B already. Instead, he paged over to another video. It was also a recording from his own system, only it had been made years ago, long before he had even heard of the Cubicle Men. He'd often thought that it was a good thing that video was all software now, because otherwise he'd have watched this footage until it fell apart. He spent the night slugging from his bottle of Best and watching it again. By the time he took a hit of SleepingJuice and fell into his narrow bed, he was glad that he'd picked up another bottle of rum.

# THREE

DEX AWOKE TO the familiar throb of a headache and he tasted a gummy film in his mouth. He reached over to the small shelf next to the bed for the large bottle of Flying Fish Tonix. He drank a large gulp and fought the brief flash of nausea that followed. In a moment the headache was dulled and he got up. After stepping into the lavatory cubicle, he turned on the spray and showered quickly. When he was done, the bathroom's ceiling nozzle began to dry him and the room and he brushed his teeth and used the toilet.

He pulled his uniform out of the autoclave and put it on, stuffing a nutrient bar into the pocket. He was out the door and on his way to work in less than ten minutes after the alarm went off. The sky was its usual grey and there were only patches of it visible between the tops of the building. Dex wasn't looking at the sky, though. He had already logged into the Cubicle Men's system and was paging through the overnight news. There were the usual attacks on streeters that the goon squad busted up, a few domestic cases among the "differently employed" and what looked like a very interesting case in Asia of a missing piece of artwork. Obviously, the client had acquired it though less than honest means originally. Dex thought he would have liked that one.

Dex scanned over the list of ongoing cases for his squad as he boarded the train, one eye on the scrolling text and the other on a local news board. He stood on the train, sardined in with the other commuters, while he got a sense of what was going on with the other Cubicle Men in the city. As a lieutenant, Dex had a part time responsibility as a mentor for the other members. Lieutenant was really the highest rank anyone achieved and still was on active duty. After lieutenant it was all administration and recruiting, something in which Dex had less than zero interest.

When he really thought about it, Dex knew that he wasn't an ambitious man, so it didn't bother him that he was never going to rise any further. The organization, although technically hierarchical in structure, didn't really place a lot of status on the various ranks. It was more focussed on finding the right niche for each member. Consider Buster Takahashi. He'd been a goon before Dex started and he was still there, cracking heads, busting ribs and putting the fear of death into people with the best of them. He'd never get off the street and he'd never get past constable, either. But he was one of the most respected guys in the squad, he was so damn good at what he did.

Dex knew he wasn't in Buster's league, but he also knew that he was good at his job. He had one of the higher solve rates in the squad and he truly liked his work. Although most of the other Ds in the squad wouldn't have pegged him as an introspective guy, Dex had thought a lot about what made him good at this kind of work. He had never been great at school, in fact he'd always been pretty average at everything he had tried. He was stubborn, though, and once he sunk his teeth into something he had a hell of a time letting go. But, the only real aptitude he'd ever shown was for talking to people, making friends - although that was all in the past now.

Dex shook his head slightly, as though shaking the thoughts loose. There was no point in dwelling on that; he had real work to do. The train slowed and Dex's onboard system showed a reminder superimposed over his vision that this was his stop. He pushed through the crowd to the door and stepped out. He walked the block to the B&B offices, still reading over the local Cubicle Men cases. He logged out just before passing through the doors to the Customer Service Reps' room. He knew that B&B's system would scan him as he entered, logging his time in and ensuring that we wasn't using company time for non-work-related lollygagging.

However, once he was at his workstation, waving his hands over the B&B interface to check his messages and log in to the call system, he ran a program from his own system that allowed him to access the external parts of everywherenet without the B&B system noticing the additional traffic. This way, Dex could work on his real work while doing the job that paid the bills and kept him housed. As he answered the first complaint of the day, Dex saw that he had a text message from Ivy waiting for him. He paged over to it and while going through the motions with the B&B customer, he read through her message.

She claimed that she hadn't been able to come up with a lot of information about the Reuben identity, since most of it was housed in his own memory cells, which had been destroyed. She did give a timeline from her own memory, though. She said she'd created Reuben about five years previously, first as a purely textual identity for some boards she posted at and for an online journal. The journal had been automatically deleted when Reuben had been killed, but Ivy said it was just a collection of essays about user interface issues. After she'd been using the Reuben identity for a year or so, she set about creating an avatar for him in the visual interface to everywherenet.

"It was harder than I thought it would be," she wrote. "M City piggybacks on the identity system for the everywherenet itself, rather than having its own user management system like the boards do. I had to create a complete identity within a shell inside my own system. It was tough, but after a few months of solid work, I had it working.

"Reuben was, in a very real sense, a complete individual. He had access to the everywherenet as if he were entirely separate from Ivy - it got to the point where I could switch back and forth between the two identities very easily. Technically speaking, that is. It's funny - the easier it became to master the technology, the harder it was to actually switch personalities myself."

After she described her technological achievement, Ivy explained that she had originally created the Reuben identity because she was involved in a community that was devoted to discussion issues of privacy and anonymity on the 'nets. She posted occasionally to their boards and developed an alternate identity, as most of the posters there did. Once she created an avatar for the Marionette City interface, though, the Reuben identity became more fully formed and she began to use it more often in the virtual world. She made reference to using Reuben for some freelance work and Dex made a note to find out more about that.

Dex had finished with his first call of the work day at B&B and was now helping another customer install a new disk node. He figured that he could take care of that call in his sleep, so he continued to mull over the information in Ivy's note. It was a start, but there were several questions he'd asked her that were notable in the absence of answers.

He had asked her if anyone knew she had a multi and she'd completely ignored that rather important question. Since the avatar was attacked with code, Dex was starting with the premise that Reuben's killer had known that Reuben was a multi, but was it a deliberate act against Reuben/Ivy, or was it simply a statement against multis in general? Without more information from Ivy, Dex wouldn't even know where to start. He sent her a message asking her to meet him in the bar again later that day to address some questions. He had to focus on the unhappy B&B customers for much longer than he would have preferred before he got a reply agreeing to his time.

• • •

Dex arrived first. It was his habit to link in to the bar a good half hour before his client was due to meet him. He liked to be able to see the client arrive - you could tell a lot about the way the meeting was going to go from those first few moments. But Dex also happened to like this place; it was dark, with a blue and green light show over the main area. The tables at the sides, where Dex liked to sit, were in barely enough light to see across the table. No one would be peeking in on a conversation there. The bar streamed music and Dex enjoyed the stuff they played. It wasn't the garbage that was currently popular and it set a nice atmosphere. Of course, you could always change to your own soundtrack or turn the sound off entirely, but Dex liked the effort they put in to the music and the ambience of the place. It felt comfortable. As comfortable as an online gin joint ever could feel to him.

Dex watched the other patrons while his avatar worked on a drink. If he had wanted to, he could have had his system replicate the effects on his physical body, but he'd rather taste his drugs as they went in. He just liked the look of his avatar with a drink in its hand. He changed his perspective to be able to look at his avatar from a cinematic view. He had designed it to look more or less like his physical body did, without all the metal nodes dotting his face. It wore a dark suit of an somewhat anachronistic style, which fit with the compact but wide body. The head was shaved almost bald, but a close observer could just make out the line of dark grey stubble at the base of his skull under his old fashioned hat. The avatar's dark eyes closed briefly as it brought the drink to its thin lips and took a long swallow.

Dex knew he could have built an avatar that would have been more attractive or fanciful and many people's avatars were of that ilk. But he never thought to embellish; it just seemed unnecessary. Secretly, he thought the suit and hat were a bit of an indulgence, but no one had ever commented. He reset his view back to first person and waited for Ivy to show up.

This time she linked directly in to the bar, her avatar materializing in an empty area of the open space in the middle of the room. The light show played on her rendering form, first cutting through her image, then bouncing off the dress and skin. She took a moment to get her bearings, then scanned the faces, looking for Dex. He sent her a private audio message indicating where he was and she walked over to the table. She sat without waiting for an invitation and this time ordered a drink from the bartender software.

Dex didn't stand on ceremony. "I got your message," he said. "And there's some information missing. If you want me to find out what happened to him, I'm going to need to know everything about Reuben. Why you created him, who knew him, who knew about his connection with you, all of it." He paused, but Ivy just sipped her drink and held his gaze. "I know this is difficult, but you have to help me before I can help you. And if you don't want my help, there's a hundred other people who do. So, don't waste my fucking time."

Ivy didn't say anything for a moment and Dex wondered if she was just going to link out of the bar and that would be the end of the case. He hoped she would stay, because the case intrigued him, but he had nothing to go on unless she could give him more information. His avatar kept its stoic expression, but Dex's physical face smiled when Ivy started to talk.

"No one knew about Reuben and me," she said, quietly. "There was nothing to link us. I never told anyone about Reuben until yesterday, when I told you." She looked at Dex defiantly, as if daring him to question her. He softened the look on his avatar's face and she dropped her eyes. "This is very hard for me," she said, her voice almost a whisper. "I got so used to keeping it a secret, that even saying my-" she caught herself. "Even saying his name out loud seems, terrifying."

"It's okay," Dex said, his avatar's expression kindly while in the physical world he rolled his eyes and sighed. "But we need to talk about Reuben if you want me to help you. What were you dong when you were using that identity? Who were you talking to, what communities were you in and what were those freelance projects all about?" He swallowed the last of his drink and refilled the glass. Ivy lifted her own glass and followed suit.

"Fine," she said, lifting her eyes to meet his gaze. "I hope you have some time."

# FOUR

"IT STARTED OUT of pure scientific curiosity. In case it isn't obvious," she said, "I design user interfaces for a living. I work for..." She paused. "I work for one of the bigger firms and I do pretty well. Dealing with the interaction between people and machines, you tend to end up thinking of it in one of two ways — either it's all just a programming problem, with inputs and outputs and your job is to try and make it all fit together. Or you become obsessed with the psychology of it all. And that was me.

"I started reading all these boards about human/machine interaction and not just the ones about making it work. The ones about how it makes us feel. About how it makes us more than human, less than human, something other than human. How it makes us different, how it changes our lives. Now, obviously, I didn't want to post using my real identity. I'm somewhat well known in the field and even if no one would have recognized me, I wouldn't have wanted the firm's routine scans to turn up activity at some of the boards that are hostile to our work. And so Reuben was born.

"I first used that identity on those boards, but when I started keeping a journal about my observations, it seemed obvious to use Reuben as the author. My... Reuben's pages never had a huge audience, but there were a few avid readers. The Reuben identity began to make connections within the community — he developed his own personality, his own friends. By the time I made an avatar for him, he was more popular socially than I was."

Dex wondered if he heard a trace of envy in her voice and added the thought to his running log of notes from the conversation. Aloud, he said, "Can you give me some names, people or groups I can talk to who associated with Reuben?"

Ivy swirled the liquid in her glass and seemed to be staring at it as if it, rather than she herself held the answers to Dex's questions. "Sure," she said, finally. "The only trouble is that none of them know me as Ivy. And no one knows that Reuben is... gone."

"Just get me the names," Dex said. "I can handle the rest. I've done it before."

"What will you tell them?" Ivy asked, her voice trembling slightly.

"The truth," Dex said, "that Reuben was murdered and that I'm investigating." He finished his drink and set the empty glass on the table. "Don't worry," he said, "I won't mention you. I don't even think I'll need to mention that he was a multi, at least not yet. Just let me take care of it." He could hear Ivy sigh deeply, as if she had been holding her breath the whole time and was only letting it out now.

"I'll send you contact information for everyone I can remember," Ivy said. "A lot of it was lost in Reuben's memory, but I should be able to dig up some addresses and links."

"Good," Dex said. "We'll meet again once I've had a chance to go over the list." He linked out of the bar and refocussed on the physical world.

• • •

Dex ran his tongue around his mouth and grimaced at the taste. Sometimes he was able to pay attention to his physical surroundings when he was in Marionette City, but this wasn't one of those times. He went offline, blinked a few times to readjust his vision to his apartment and drew a glass of water. He swirled the liquid around his mouth and spat onto the floor of the lav. He poured a liberal dose of rum into the glass and topped it off with ginger ale.

By the time he was back at the table and logged back into the 'nets, he had a message waiting from Ivy. It was a list of names — mostly links to boards Reuben had frequented, but a few individual names as well. Dex decided to start on the boards, since Ivy had provided little contact information for the individuals. He logged into the Cubicle Men's system and was reminded of the weekly squad meeting the next day. He sent the names Ivy had given him to the organization's database with a request to have the results sent directly to him. Then he paged over to the first board Ivy had sent him.

It was one of the communities Ivy had described. Dex scanned the board and decided that the denizens seemed to be mostly a bunch of pseudo-intellectuals pontificating about things they don't really know a lot about. Dex read a few of the most recent posts, then looked up Reuben's posts. The items tagged to Reuben seemed to Dex to be on the less controversial side, mostly asking questions, or looking for insight. It didn't seem to be a terribly personal board; the interactions more on topic and pretending to be academic. Dex found boards like that to be unbelievably boring, so he moved on.

Most of the links Ivy had given him were to similar areas, though Dex found a couple of boards where the conversation was more like a group of friends than a philosophy conference. Boring, pedantic friends, but friends none the less. Dex spent more time reading the posts on these boards, learning a bit about Reuben's relationships with these people and noting who seemed to be closest to him. Reuben didn't seem to be involved in any great arguments here either, but Dex knew that the relationships formed on a board could easily spill over to socializing in Marionette City or even, in extreme cases, the physical world.

He poured another drink and pulled up his credentials file. Inside, he had what appeared to be certified keys for a couple of false identities — mostly as a member of Security for the larger firms. They wouldn't stand up to any kind of rigorous scrutiny, but they usually got him in the door. This time, though, he thought it might be better to make it clear that he was an independent. The Cubicle Men didn't exist officially, but everyone had heard of them one way or another. It was just a question of making it clear who he was without having to answer too many questions. Dex chose the signature file that was closest to the truth — Andersson Dexter, independent investigator of private claims and concerns.

Dex spent the next hour sending messages to Reuben's friends from the boards, informing them of Reuben's unfortunate death and explaining that he was investigating and would like to talk to them.

He attached the signature file and hoped that at least a few people would respond. With the messages sent, he checked to see if the database had come up with any information about the names Ivy had given him. He got a few leads and saw that for a couple of the names there were surprisingly long dossiers in the database. He decided to learn a bit more about these individuals before tipping them off quite yet.

• • •

The two most interesting reads belonged to two files — people calling themselves Alvaro Zuccarelli and Tequila Kate. Zuccarelli was well known to the Cubicle Men, his file indicating that he was one of the gainfully unemployed — someone who made a living without working for one of the firms. He had previously employed the Cubicle Men to resolve a business dispute — a client had skived off without paying the bill. Dex scrolled through the document and saw that while Zuccarelli was certainly living a life off the grid, he seemed to be legitimate. There was no indication that he had ever been investigated for anything and his account with the organization had been fully paid in full and on time.

Tequila Kate, on the other hand, didn't ring any bells for Dex except the obvious one that she must be a corker at parties. It turned out that the name was not exactly a terrible pseudonym, as Dex had assumed, but rather that Kate was essentially an activist for the cause of people with multiple identities. She was a self-identified multi, though no one knew who her creator was and she had a popular and controversial journal about the benefits of multiple identities and the struggle to have their rights identified. The dossier provided links to a couple of boards that were unavailable through regular searches of the 'nets and Dex paged over to check them out. They all required separate authentication, then a moderator had to approve the application for access. Obviously, they wanted to avoid the anti-multi trolls on the boards. Dex figured he could bluff his way past the mod, but he wasn't interested in waiting so he pinged Annabelle Lewis, the squad's resident cracker. The word around the squad was that there wasn't anywhere on the 'nets Annabelle couldn't find her way into. After a brief conversation, she promised to get him in to the boards, but it wouldn't last long. Dex told her he wouldn't need long and thanked her for the help. Only five minutes later she pinged him with the login details. Once he'd gained access, he set a script to download a complete archive of each board to his personal system. He guessed that their security wouldn't be expecting anyone to try that, since it would eat a lot of disk. Dex, of course, had plenty and he planned to delete anything that wasn't interesting anyway.

While the download was starting to come down and his head was only beginning to throb, Dex paged over to Tequila Kate's journal. He searched for any reference to Reuben Cobalt, but came up blank. It seemed that while Kate was outspoken in her opinion that multis should be treated no differently than "real" identities, she was sensitive to the fact that most multis were trying to pass as first identities. Her journal rarely named other multis, preferring to refer to "a friend" or "some folks."

Dex found her posts to be surprisingly sane, but there were the telltale elements of a zealot in there. There were the obvious comparisons between the plight of multis to the historical struggles of race and gender equality, but she also advocated that everyone take up a separate identity. It was obvious that she not only believed that her choices were as good as any other, but that they were, in fact, superior.

Dex was scanning one of Kate's many articles articles about the merits of separate identities to correspond with different aspects of one's personality, when he felt the familiar wave of nausea. He closed his eyes as the final weight of the download came upon him, then it was over. He paged over to the files he'd just received from the private boards and ran a scan for Reuben Cobalt. There were hits. Rather a lot of hits, in fact. Dex had his system aggregate just those posts and display them. Reuben had been a regular poster at both boards, at the support board first, then more frequently and more recently at the other board.

It was devoted to services for multis — tools to create realistic logins, information on how to hide your multi from friends and family, the usual underground stuff. Reuben's posts were easy to find. It looked like his services were in quite a heavy demand. Reuben was selling the code to build multiple avatars for use in Marionette City.

• • •

"You have withheld key information from me." Dex was using his goon voice, though he wasn't anywhere near as angry as he sounded. "How do you expect me to help you if you won't tell me anything?" He left the words just hanging there, waiting for Ivy to answer. He wished he could have seen her face, but she wasn't logged in to Marionette City when he checked and he wasn't willing to wait for her.

"Do you have any idea what would happen to me if it came out that I was selling a way to essentially hack M City?" Ivy's voice was small and timid and Dex could tell that this conversation was hard for her.

"Of course," he answered, shortly. "At best you would be fired and never get work at another firm again. You'd probably be sued out of any savings you've got. You'd almost certainly end up on the streets and I honestly don't fancy your chances of making it a year out there. At worst..." He paused, as if thinking. "Well, who cares about how much worse it could get? But how could you think I wouldn't find this out? Did you really think you could hide this from me and actually get a successful investigation? Are you insane as well as stupid?"

Ivy was silent and Dex wondered if he had gone too far. Eventually, he heard an intake of breath and her voice came back, surprisingly clear. "No," she said. "Just stupid. It's a habit to hide these things; I've been doing it for a while, you know."

"Well you've got to stop," Dex said, bluntly. "At least with me. You've already trusted me with enough information to utterly ruin your life and you have to just keep on trusting me. This won't work otherwise." He softened his voice, trying to sound sympathetic. If they had been meeting in Marionette City he would have reached out to touch her hand or arm, something to make it seem like he cared about her as a person, not just the puzzle of the case. "So talk to me. Tell me what you know."

"I don't know anything," she said, her voice quivering. "I just don't understand why. Why would someone do this? Who could hate me this much?" She finally broke down and Dex could hear her sobs.

He let her cry and when he could barely hear her ragged breath, he said, "That's exactly what I'm trying to find out. And that's what I need you to tell me."

# FIVE

TO HEAR HER tell it, she was the only person Dex had ever met who didn't have an enemy in the world. Of course, there were all those people who believed that multis were a threat to commerce and society and needed to be banished from the 'nets. But other than them, Ivy was loved and admired by all.

Dex was getting tired of it; hell, he was just plain getting tired. He finally told her to send him a list of everyone she talked with socially and he promised to be discreet if he had to talk to them. For once she went one better and gave him the list right then and there. It was short, though. Just three names — Bill Christo, Renna Bellinger and Julie Abrentz.

"Please don't tell them," Ivy asked. "You don't even need to talk to them. They doesn't know anything about it. We've never even talked about multis before."

"How do you all know each other?"

"I met Bill and Julie through Renna."

"And what about her?" Dex asked.

"She works in another branch of my firm," Ivy said, "She's a UI designer, like me."

"So you work together?"

"No," Ivy said, "we met through work, but we don't work together. We're," she paused, as if looking for the right word. "We're friends. That's all. I don't want her mixed up in this, it's just not fair to her."

"I told you I'd be discreet," Dex said, "but if I have to talk to these people, I will. You just have to trust me." Ivy reluctantly agreed and ended the conversation. Dex added the new information to his notes and poured another drink. It had been a long night and he had another long shift at B&B the next day. But he figured he had enough time to watch a quick video.

• • •

Maksym was lying on the couch, a cigarette in one hand and a drink in the other. There was music playing, loud enough that they had to speak up in order to talk. Maks had his eyes closed, his head slightly bobbing in time to the music as he sang along. This was Dex's favourite part. The part where they sang along, the way a person might in the lav, loud and off key and perfectly happy. He saw Maks take a drag of the contraband cigarette and the smoke curled up over his head as he sang. Dex remembered that he had sung too and he could sometimes make out the sound of his own voice on the video.

He stilled the image, searched his archive for the song they had been listening to and played it. He sat, sipping his rum and ginger and looked at Maksym's still face, frozen in song. The song ended, but Dex just sat there for a moment. Then, he took the bottle of SleepingJuice, drank a six hour dose and fell into bed.

• • •

Dex awoke still dressed and feeling as bad as he usually did first thing in the morning. After taking a hit of Flying Fish, ditching his sweaty, wrinkled clothes in the autoclave and spending five minutes in the lav, he felt almost human again. He rode the train into B&B while eating a nutrient bar and checking in on the previous night's news.

At his work station, he logged into the backdoor and checked his personal messages. Amazingly, a few of the people he'd contacted the previous day from Ivy's list had answered. They all expressed the same shock and horror at Reuben's death and offered any help they could. Good. Dex could finally get some kind of a clue about what Reuben was like. He didn't trust Ivy's assessment one bit, she was just too close. And by her own admission, she wasn't exactly a social butterfly — her perceptions of people easily could be skewed.

He started with the first response, from someone called Sterling Ljundberg. Dex's assigned shift at B&B that day was answering text inquiries, so he was able to send a voice request to Ljundberg. He set his system to process subvocal input, so the conversation would be silent at his end, but translated to audio at the receiving end. Ljundberg answered and Dex introduced himself.

"Oh, yes, Mister Dexter," the voice at the other end said, somewhat obsequiously, "if that's the correct way to address you..."

"Just Dex is fine," he answered. "I wanted to talk to some of the people who knew Reuben, to get a sense of the man. I'm particularly interested in finding out if you have any idea who might have had a grudge..." Dex let the end of the sentence linger, waiting for Ljundberg to fill the empty space.

"It's just so shocking," the other man finally said. "I mean, Reuben was such a nice guy. I know that sounds rather, well, lame, I suppose. But in this case it's just the best way to describe him. He was genuinely nice. He wasn't like the trolls you get on the boards, he wasn't even one of those people who get all excited if someone challenges their opinion. He was just a plain old good guy. I can't believe that someone would murder him. That's just insane."

Some people would argue that murder was always insane, Dex thought, but aloud he said, "So, you can't think of anyone who had it in for Reuben, anyone who specifically didn't get along with him?"

"No," Ljundberg said. "He's not- I mean he wasn't the kind of person who made enemies. He never got into fights, hardly even got into heated debates. Though I can't imagine that anyone on the boards people like us frequented would kill anyone, even if they hated each other. We're, well, we're intellectuals. We use words, not..." His voice trailed off. "Say, how was Reuben killed?"

Dex knew this would come eventually and he'd already decided to just go with the truth. "Well, it's a little complicated," he said. "You see, Reuben Cobalt was an alternate identity." Dex heard Ljundberg draw his breath in sharply. "He was killed by code."

"My god," Ljundberg said. "A multi? But, I... we... he never said anything; I never knew." There was silence for a while. "Is that really, I mean, do you still call this a murder? Or is Reuben's...

creator dead, too?"

"No," Dex said, "though I can't say anything else about that."

"No, I would think not. A multi. That explains a few things." Ljundberg seemed almost to have forgotten that he was speaking to another person.

"Such as?" Dex prompted.

"Oh. Well, how do I put it? He was private, I guess. Though, no more than many of us, I suppose."

"How do you mean, 'private'?" Dex asked. "What made you think that?"

"Well," Ljundberg said, "From what I can remember, he never mentioned where he lived. There was a discussion about where we were all from one day and he was notable in his absence from that conversation. I remember wondering if he was still on the board, but then he showed up again in a different conversation. And he never talked about his past. Of course, he never posted any images of himself either, but like I said, none of this is terribly strange, really. But it makes sense now, I guess a different kind of sense. We're all presenting a particular face to one another here, I suppose. I wonder how many of us really have separate identities when we're online, practically speaking, whether we know it or not?"

Dex figured the conversation wasn't going to get anywhere useful at this stage; it must just be a hazard of talking to amateur philosophers. He made the usual noises asking Ljundberg to let him know if he thought of anything that might be helpful. Dex then said that he was sorry to be the bearer of bad news and gave Ljundberg his typical end of interview speech. He made a few notes and moved on to the next name on the list.

Ginette De Moranville had the same non-story to tell, though at least she had a charming accent to tell it in. Dex was surprised to hear an accent — he thought they were all but extinct and only found in historical entertainment vids. De Moranville explained that her parents had been eccentric history buffs and had brought her up speaking French. She'd apparently had a horrible time in school, although it had enabled lucrative careers in voice work and interpretation and translation for historians. Like Ljundberg, De Moranville was shocked at Reuben's death and also professed ignorance at his being an alternate identity. She seemed nonplussed by the revelation, though, and in between possibly false sobs, she kept repeating, "Mon dieu, pauvre Reuben."

Aside from the language lesson, Dex's conversation with her was just as fruitless as his talk with Ljundberg. While he felt it would likely be a continued waste of time, Dex was nothing if not thorough, so he called the last name on his list. Mickey Udo was unavailable, but his messenger told Dex what time Udo would be in Marionette City. The program even provided a link, which Dex noted. He ought to be able to look up Udo after the squad meeting that evening.

Meanwhile, Dex decided it was time to talk to some of the people who were involved more intimately with Reuben Cobalt. His business associates. Dex pulled up the contact information for Alvaro Zuccarelli and pinged him using the independent investigator identity. He figured Zuccarelli would know exactly who Dex worked with, if not why he was calling. As he expected, Zuccarelli answered almost immediately.

"Andersson Dexter," a smooth voice said. "Lieutenant, I believe. What can I do for you today?"

Dex was surprised that the man knew enough about the Cubicle Men to identify his rank, but he decided to just go with it. "Correct, Mr. Zuccarelli. But, you have the advantage of me, I'm afraid."

"How so?"

"You seem to know a great deal about me, but all I know about you is that you've done some business with someone I want to know a little more about."

"And who might that be?"

"Reuben Cobalt."

"Hmm," the silky voice said. "The name doesn't ring a bell. In what context would I have encountered Mr. Cobalt?"

"Well, that's more or less what I was hoping to find out from you, Mr. Zuccarelli." Dex was being a trifle disingenuous, since Ivy had explained that Zuccarelli had essentially been Reuben's banker. A multi that was functioning independently needed a way to pay for things and as it turned out, Reuben had an income as well. But all financial transactions were tied to a person's everywherenet authentication, as well as an individual bank account. Ivy's system could fake the authentication, but it didn't come with a built in bank account. Enter Alvaro Zuccarelli.

"I'm sorry that I can't be of more assistance, Lieutenant. Perhaps if you allow me to check my records, I may be able to find some information my inferior brain has forgotten." Zuccarelli was going out of his way to be an ass now, Dex figured, since he highly doubted that there were any records the man couldn't have accessed while they talked. Still, he'd go on playing it nice. For now.

"I'd be very grateful for any help you could provide, Mr. Zuccarelli," Dex said, his voice almost betraying the contempt he felt. He ended the call and went on a break. He visited the toilet and then headed to B&B's break room for a coffee. When he got back to his work station, he addressed a few more complaints and scanned over the agenda for the weekly squad meeting that evening. He wondered what Zuccarelli was hiding. Being Reuben's banker was no big deal and Dex was sure that Zuccarelli's personal experience with the Cubicle Men would have made it crystal clear that Dex wouldn't care about that. Maybe it was pure professionalism — Dex imagined that part of the package was anonymity and though he figured that usually would end when the client died, maybe it didn't for Zuccarelli's operation. More out of habit than for any real reason, he played the recording of the conversation back to himself at double speed, while he answered a few enquiries for B&B customers. He was in the middle of copying and pasting a section of the instruction manual for one hapless customer when it dawned on him that he'd never gotten around to telling Zuccarelli that his client was, indeed, dead.

On the upside, Dex figured that having that bit of data still in hand might make the bad cop version of the conversation go a little smoother — at his end, anyway. He finished up his last few bits and pieces for B&B and logged out of all systems before heading out the door. The reader in the doorway logged him out, as well as thoroughly but ineffectually scanning him for any extracurricular system activity. Once he was through the door, he linked into Marionette City and while his body was headed home, his avatar headed off to the office.

# SIX

DEX WALKED INTO the squad room and nodded at the familiar faces. Dex thought that the weekly squad meetings were unnecessary in many ways, but he had to admit that once in a while he needed skills he just didn't have and it helped to have an informal relationship with the people you were asking for help. Thinking about his deficiencies in the realm of programming, he found a chair next to Annabelle, who asked him if the boards she cracked for him had given him what he needed. "Dunno," he said and she got a worried look on her face. "No, your part worked fine," he said, "I just don't know how useful it's going to be. This case is a bit of a stumper."

"How so?" Annabelle asked and Dex explained that there wasn't a lot of information about the victim since he was really just a bunch of code and it was all scrambled now. "Another one of those multis," she said, disgust in her voice. Dex raised an eyebrow, but said nothing. She looked up at Dex and her voice changed back to its usual, light, helpful tone. "I can take a look at what's left for you," she offered. Dex thanked her, saying that he would keep it in mind. Her voice lowered. "I'm always available for you," she said and Dex ignored the significant look she was giving him.

Everyone in the squad knew that Annabelle had a serious thing for Dex, but if he noticed he was good at hiding it. Captain Zahara Zhang, known to the squad as Zizou, took her spot in front of the group and the informal chatter quieted. She had recently been promoted from the detectives' ranks and the switch to admin was a natural one for her. The squad all liked and respected her and so far she had done a good job of keeping the gears oiled.

"Okay gang," she said, "let's keep it brief. There's not a lot to report from my end; we've had a few new cases for the Ds, mostly extortion and some kind of murder-like thing. Ask Dex about that one if you're interested." He got a handful of pings immediately and just pointed them all back to his public case file. They could read his preliminary report just as well as they could ask him about the case and it didn't cost him hours of telling the same story over and over again.

"The street guys have seen an slight increase in activity in green and brown sectors this week." The captain used the squad's terminology for a couple of the more down and out neighbourhoods in the city. She continued, "So we're adding an extra unit for those areas. Anyone have any info on why there's more trouble?" The captain scanned the crowd and a hand in the back went up. It was Melissa Vonruden, one of the new goons. "Go ahead," Zizou said.

Vonruden stood up and in a strong voice said, "Sir, I think it might be because of a new joint in that area offering neural stimulants. Just on this side of legal, I think."

"You working green or brown, officer?" the captain asked.

"No, sir," Vonruden flushed. "My day job is at the stim joint's front counter." The squad laughed at her embarrassment and the captain smiled.

"Good work, officer. Check in with Malone and let him know what you know." The captain paused, likely checking notes, then continued. "Anyone have anything else they need to share?" There were a few murmurs but no one stood to take the floor. "Okay then. Street, you'll get the week's assignments from Malone. Ds, if anyone is bored, let me know and we'll find something to put you on. Otherwise, dismissed."

The group broke up, a few people chatting and the goon squad crowding around Pat Malone to work out the week's schedule. As he was leaving, Dex nodded at Jay Shiraishi, a guy he'd worked with when he was still on the goon squad, who was talking with Annabelle. As he passed them, Annabelle said, "A few of us are heading over to Monte's for a pint or several before calling it a day. Want to come with?"

"No can do," Dex said. "This meeting took up enough of my time already. I've got a date with one of my vic's old buddies. Hopefully he'll be more useful than the others have been. I'll catch you later." He walked out of the squad room, leaving Annabelle to link over to the bar by herself. Instead of linking over to his own destination, Dex walked through Marionette City toward the point where Mickey Udo had said he'd be.

Dex liked to walk through Marionette City — it reminded him of a time in his life when he used to go for walks in the physical world. Much of Marionette City had been modeled after the physical world as it once was, long before Dex's time. However, when Dex was young there were still a few throwbacks — bars with more than a half dozen kinds of booze, take out joints that cooked food made with real ingredients, stores that sold physical things that were more than just add ons for a person's system.

The squad meetings were held in a part of Marionette City called Chandlers. It usually rained and it was always twilight and the designer had put these funky shadows everywhere that didn't actually relate to any of the objects. Dex liked it there. According to the link Udo had given him, he was going to be in a location that was directly adjacent to Chandlers. Dex had time to kill, so he pulled his hat down over his heavy eyebrows and set to walking.

Chandlers was overstocked with bars, whorehouses, numbers rackets and backalley bankers. A man could hock his next paycheque for a loan and spend the lot on random number generators, teledildonic hookers and virtual hooch. These were common enough pastimes and there were plenty of punters in each doorway. Places like this kept the Cubicle Men busy and Dex felt at home here. He was tempted to stop in at one of the ginmills along the way, but he didn't want to miss Udo so he kept up the pace.

He was out of Chandlers soon enough and into a more typical part of Marionette City. It was animated in a lighter style that originated in Asia, Annabelle had told him once. Dex didn't know anything about that and was neither a historian nor a designer. All he knew was that he looked and felt out of place here. He found his way through the winding streets, bubble-shaped buildings and avatars with exaggerated features and fantastic extremities like wings or tentacles. Dex entered the lounge where Udo said he'd be and pinged the man. Udo answered and Dex saw a figure waving from the back of the room.

Udo's avatar was at a table near the far wall, with a bowl of some steaming thing in front of him. Dex couldn't tell if it was supposed to be food or a drug and hoped that whatever it was wouldn't affect the interview. He sat across from Udo and introduced himself.

"You're here about Reuben, right?" Udo asked, shifting the steaming bowl to one side.

Dex cut to the chase. "Can you tell me anything about him, anything that might help me figure out who killed him?"

"I don't know," Udo said, looking sad. "It's such a shock. I saw him only last week..." His voice trailed off and Dex wondered if he was hiding something or just lost in memory.

"You saw him..." Dex prompted.

"Yes," Udo answered, "We used to go to this bar near here." He cocked his head, indicating a direction to his right. "One of the local strip places — all amateur hour, you know. Lots of wings and feathers."

"Sure," Dex said. "Any trouble there?"

Udo laughed. "Like, Reuben took a shine to a particular dancer and it ended badly? Hardly. Reuben liked to watch, sure, but it was never like that. I think he liked the sense of freedom they had up there, looking however they wanted to and showing it off."

"He said this to you?" Dex asked.

"Not in so many words," Udo said. "But I knew Reuben wasn't turned on by them. Or at least not by any individual one of them." He leaned toward Dex, his eyes clamped on to Dex's. "I think he got off on by the whole idea. That they can have wings, or blue skin or whatever they want. He was turned on by the possibility." He looked at Dex for a moment longer, then turned back to the stage.

Dex was silent for a while. "Did you know Reuben was a multi?" he eventually asked.

Udo closed his eyes and bowed his head. "He never said anything, if that's what you mean. But, yeah, I figured as much."

"How?" Dex asked, leaning forward.

"I've known a few of them," Udo said, uncharacteristically circumspect. "He fit the type. And one night, I kinda brought it up."

"You asked him if he was a multi?" Dex said.

"Not straight out like that," Udo said, as if Dex were an idiot for thinking that. "Just started talking about the concept, you know, let him know that I'm friends with a few and that it's all cool. He didn't rise to the bait and pretty soon after that he got busy all of a sudden. We used to hang out a couple of times a week and we were usually on the same boards the rest of the time. Then, he started making excuses to skip out on me and he was hardly ever on the boards. At first I thought he was just taking a break or getting into something else," Udo shrugged. "The same old stuff can get dull after awhile; we all need new things every once and again. But when we did hang out, he seemed distracted and, I don't know, kind of upset. I asked what was up a few times, but he just gave me the brush off. I figured he just wasn't ready to talk about it."

Udo looked off into space for a while and said, "Hang on, though. I think I remember something from around then that might be useful. Let me check." Udo's avatar was stock still for a moment, then it shook back to life. "Got it!" Udo said. "We were at the Lucky Eleven — that's the bar — and we ran into this girl that Reuben knew. He seemed to be kind of weird about seeing her there, at the time I wondered if they were fucking or something. I've got vid of it, if you want it."

"You have vid?" Dex asked, surprised. As a rule, most people didn't record their lives in the kind of detail that Dex did.

"Yeah," Udo said, grinning. "Maybe Reuben didn't have the hots for the dancers, but I sure do."

Dex smiled, saying, "Fair enough. Mind if I take a copy?"

"By all means," Udo said. "I don't know if it means anything, but at the very least if they were fucking, she ought to be told that he's, you know, gone." Udo pinged Dex and he authorized the transfer.

"Thanks," Dex said, feeling the weight in his head increase just slightly.

"No problem," Udo said. "And, if you're into that kind of thing, I'd recommend you check out the third dancer in." He whistled low and cocked an eyebrow. "Very hot."

Dex shook his head, chuckling to himself and he linked out of the bar.

• • •

He poured a shot of Jamaica's Best and topped it off with a splash of gingapop and checked the time. Between both jobs, he'd worked a long day today and though he knew he should take a look at Udo's vid, Dex wanted a few minutes for himself. He sat in his comfortable chair, resting the drink on its arm. He fired up his full screen viewer and loaded a different video.

He hadn't started recording his life all the time when this video was taken, so he had missed the beginning. But even though it was a long time ago, Dex remembered walking to the bar as clearly as if it were on the video, he'd made the trip so many times. The door was nondescript, just another metal door in just another slightly dilapidated building in the wrong part of town. You had to know what to look for to see the initials J.T. scratched into the surface of the door at eye level. Dex had known.

The video started inside J.T.'s, with Dex and two of his friends at the usual table in the corner. The sound was a little off — Dex hadn't perfected his recording set up yet, but he kind of liked the off-kilter resonance of the video. The music in the bar was loud enough to create a lively atmosphere, but quiet enough for the patrons to be able to carry on conversations without having to shout. That didn't necessarily stop them, however.

Dex watched his old buddy Jennie slap her hand on the table as she made her point. She always got good-naturedly argumentative after a couple of J.T.'s stiff drinks and this night was no exception. She had found a sparring companion in Dex's friend and roommate Maksym and the two were just getting started as the recording began.

"Are you crazy, Maks?" Jennie asked, her voice getting loud as it always did partway through her third gin and tonic. "You really think the firms are going to let us slip under the radar forever? We're outlaws, man! Literally. We have no job, no access to services to speak of. We've got no Security to go to bat for us when the shit hits the fan. We're on the edge out here. And you can't tell me it's not in their best interests to get rid of us."

"Come on, Jen," Maks grinned. "The firms couldn't care less about a bunch of poor artists living in the dumps out here. We don't affect them in any way. Hell, I doubt they even know we exist. Why would they care, anyway?"

"You are so naïve," Jennie said derisively, swallowing the last of her drink and setting the empty glass on the table hard. She turned her head toward the bar and grinned at the J.T., the grizzled owner and barman. "Hit me again, good sir," she said and waved a crumpled bill toward the bar. She turned back to Maksym and narrowed her eyes."Of course they know about us," she continued. "We're not invisible. We use the 'nets, we're walking around. We're consuming their resources, Maks. Eating into profits." She emphasized that last word with bitterness. "But what do we provide them with, huh? Not labour. Not even our business, on the most part. Of course, they want us gone. Gone or co-opted." J.T. delivered Jennie's drink silently. She picked up the cool glass and had a long swallow. "It's just a matter of time, man," she said. "It's all going to end. Isn't that right, Andersson?"

"Oh, no," Dex said, holding his hands up in a gesture of surrender. "I'm not getting in the middle of this."

"Come on, Andy," Maks said, slapping Dex on the back. "And miss all this fun?" Jennie snorted, but was unable to hold back a grin.

"Hey, you guys," J.T. shouted from behind the bar. "You gonna gab all night or are you gonna play already?"

"All right, all right," Jennie answered. "Keep your shorts on, man." She put her drink down and pulled a small handheld terminal from under her chair. Dex and Maksym got their instruments from under the table. The three set up their equipment on the small stage and in a few minutes were playing for the small crowd in the bar, as they did every Thursday night. Dex on mandolin, Maks on guitar and Jennie on beats, synth and mix, they filled the small bar with music for a couple of hours.

As always when he watched this recording, Dex felt his fingers move on the arm of his chair in time with those of his image. He let the video play until they were done the last set, then he switched it off. He got up and paced around his small room for moment. Then, with a sad smile, he poured another drink and settled back into his chair.

# SEVEN

DEX PAGED OVER to the file Udo had sent him. It was a good hour's worth of recording, but Dex figured he'd just skip through the dancers. Extra dangly bits didn't do it for him and when you'd seen one naked freak you'd pretty much seen them all. He scanned ahead past the floor show to the break where the dancers were just walking around the bar looking for extra cash. This would be the first time Dex would get to see Reuben alive, as it were, so he set the playback to regular speed.

He was tall and thin, with a wiry frame that would have probably held a decent amount of strength in a physical body. Dex had known more than a few goons built like that and they'd been the meanest, most bloodthirsty fighters. He'd always figured it for skinny guy syndrome. Reuben didn't carry himself like a fighter, though. Unsurprisingly, he was beautifully dressed, in slim black pants and a snug shirt that glinted, ever so slightly, in the club's lights. He wore a long coat that reached the floor and billowed out behind him, made of an almost transparent material that glinted only a slight bit more that the shirt. It was sort of like a visible aura or halo. Not a look Dex could ever carry off, but it suited Reuben.

The hair was the only thing Dex came close to envying. Short, not quite as short as his own, but very short still and silver, with an amazing luminescence. On another man it would have been overkill, or just plain silly looking, but it took Reuben out of the ordinary and made him stand out, even in this room full of avatars built to be started at. Dex had to admit, Ivy had some talent.

The recording was from Udo's personal system, so it saw what he saw. Udo was clearly most heavily focussed on the dancers, but in the break he spent more time looking at and talking with Reuben. The conversation started with comments on the various dancers' bizarre body shapes, Udo asking Reuben how certain improbable forms could be made. It was beyond boring to Dex, but he was more interested in Reuben's mannerisms. According to Udo, he had become more skittish by the time of this recording and the man's attention certainly seemed to be elsewhere. At one point in a lack-luster debate about the definition of reality, Dex noticed Reuben's face change, the eyes narrowing and lips pursing together tightly. Dex recalled Ivy's avatar, how it seemed to react the way a physical person did and wondered if she used a similar interface when she was online as Reuben.

As he watched the recording Dex could see Reuben's focus change from Udo to something over his shoulder. Udo obviously hadn't noticed whatever his friend had, since he continued to look ahead and prattle on about his point. Eventually, though, whatever had caught Reuben's attention must have approached the pair, because Udo stopped talking mid-sentence and turned around.

She was beautiful, tall, buxom, with impossible curves. All in all, she looked just like eighty percent of the female avatars in Marionette City, though in this place her commonness caused her to stand out. She smiled at Udo and then looked past him. "Reuben Cobalt," she said, cocking her head slightly. "How nice to see you again."

Reuben's face was still. So still, that Dex guessed that Ivy had purposefully disconnected any interface that would have allowed Reuben's face to automatically display whatever expression Ivy was making. "Hey, Stella," the avatar finally replied.

"Introduce me to your friend," she asked Reuben, with a sly smile on her face.

"Uh, sure." Reuben said, face still stoic. "This is Stella Bish. Stella, this is Micky Udo." They made the appropriate getting to know you noises and made small talk about the dancers. Finally, Stella stepped back.

"A little birdie told me I might find you here," she said, looking at Reuben with that smile still on her face. "You can be a tough man to find. I was hoping that we could have a little chat, but I see you're busy." She turned to Udo and favoured him with the icy but seductive smile. "I have to be going now, fellas," she said, turning to Udo, "but it was nice meeting you." She turned to Reuben and leaned in to kiss his cheek, "Now that I've found you, we'll have to talk soon, okay?"

"Sure," he said and she linked out of the lounge.

"How do you know her?" Udo asked, refocussing on the dancers as a tiny creature with wings and cat's head took the stage.

"I, uh," Reuben said, "met her through work."

"Cool," Udo said. "She seems pretty hot if you like that sort of thing," he said absently, then stopped paying attention to his friend.

Dex scanned through the rest of the vid, but there was nothing left to interest him. He ran the recording back and froze on the woman. He logged into the Cubicle Men's system and ran a search on her. The name was common and so was the avatar's appearance, so it might be tough to track her down. He let the search run and set it to send him the results. He refocussed on his room and stretched. He had stayed up later than he should have, so downed the last drops of his drink then undressed, stuffing his uniform into the autoclave.

He used the lav and took a hit of SleepingJuice. He dropped into bed and it was as if the world ceased to exist for a few hours.

• • •

Back at B&B the next day, Dex checked his messages. There were three potential matches to the Stella Bish in Udo's video and he checked them all out. The machines were pretty good at this sort of thing, but there were still some things that people did best. He'd need better computing power than the Cubicle Men could get him if he wanted a machine to accurately pick his quarry out of the line up, but Dex could tell which one he wanted just by giving the avatars the once over twice. He pinged her with the same generic message he'd sent everyone else and got on with the morning's litany of incompetent consumer complaints.

As he was handling the usual barrage of people trying to use things for purposes for which they were clearly not built, or simply not knowing where the on switch is, Dex sent a couple of messages out. One to Ivy, asking for a meeting and the other to Tequila Kate. The last was a long shot — he didn't really expect her to know all the posters at her boards — but he figured she'd be a good contact in the multi community. It was becoming more evident that not only was Ivy living two different lives, even her alter ego had things to hide from his own friends and associates.

Over the course of the day he got answers to all his enquiries and set up appointments with Ivy, Bish and even Tequila Kate. Dex was surprised when Kate answered his message so quickly and with a genuine recognition of Reuben.

"I am deeply shocked and saddened by your news of the death of such a valued member of the multi community," she wrote. "Perhaps I am being overly presumptuous, but I assume that since you are an independent and you are investigating this case, that you are aware that Reuben Colbalt was an alternate identity. If this information is news to you, I trust that it will be useful in your investigation of this heinous crime. While I do not believe that I have any information that is directly related to this incident, I am aware that seemingly innocent facts can often help lead to a successful resolution. Therefore, I welcome to opportunity to meet with you to share my remembrances of Reuben."

He spent the rest of his workday at B&B actually working on B&B work, then hightailed it home at the end of the shift. He quickly grabbed an Econoline nutrient brick and stuffed it into his mouth. While he chewed on the sticky mass, he planned ahead and just put the whole bottle of Jamaica's Best on the table before him next to his tumbler. He logged in to Marionette City just in time for his meeting with Ivy.

When Dex linked in, he saw that this time she was waiting for him, sitting at the usual table in the back of Monte's. He walked over, somewhat annoyed by the fact that he wouldn't be able to have his back to the wall. He liked to be able to see what was coming without changing out of first person view. He thought about changing his perspective to omniscient, but he wanted to be able to see Ivy's face. He could have gone with a split screen, but he found the unnaturalness of it uncomfortable, so he sucked it up and after placing his hat on the table, sat facing the wall.

"Do you have any news?" she asked, almost breathlessly.

"Not really," Dex answered, "no." Her face fell. "I've been talking with some of Reuben's associates, getting to know him, trying to find out if anyone has any information. So far, it's slow going." He checked his notes briefly, then continued. "Alvaro Zuccarelli didn't even admit to knowing Reuben."

She sighed. "I suppose I should be grateful that the anonymity he promises really exists," she said. "He knows I was behind Reuben."

"What?" Dex said, anger just about rising to the surface. "You told me no one knew Reuben was a multi."

"That's true," Ivy protested. "Zuccarelli didn't know that Reuben was a multi. Just that I was, I don't know, acting on his behalf, I guess. It was my account, just in Reuben's name."

"Right," Dex said, sighing. "Well, if Zuccarelli is as stupid as he is circumspect, I'm sure he had no idea that Reuben was your multi."

"I didn't have a choice," Ivy said, her voice getting hard. "I'm sure you don't understand. And as you saw yourself, it's not like Zuccarelli was running his mouth off, whatever he might have guessed." She was quiet for a moment, almost pouting. Dex waited. Eventually she said, "I'll tell him to talk to you." Ivy's avatar froze and Dex guessed that she was sending Zuccarelli the authorization to talk to him right then.

"Is there anyone else?" he asked, "anyone else who knows the connection between you?

"No," Ivy said, "no one. I knew Zuccarelli from... before, so it was just logical that I'd use him for Reuben. And, he's trustworthy, or more accurately, he's discreet. That's been proven."

"What do you mean, 'from before'?" Dex asked.

Ivy's eyes dropped to the table. "I'd done a little freelancing before I created Reuben. It was risky — I would have lost my job if it had become known that I was moonlighting. I met him through one of those jobs and when I realized that I needed someone to handle the finances, he seemed the obvious choice. I'd heard he was good for that." She looked up at Dex again, her face hardened. "And he was."

"Fine," Dex said. "What about Reuben's business? Client lists, that sort of thing. You must remember something."

"I've been thinking," she said, dropping her eyes again, "but I always relied on my system to remember names and contracts and so on. Well, Reuben's system. I just don't know. I've given you all the names I remember. I'm sorry."

Dex wanted to believe her, but she'd held out information from him before and he wasn't a naturally trusting fellow to begin with. However, accusing her of something wasn't going to be useful and whether she gave up all the goods or not, his bill was being paid. "Okay," he said, "I've got a few meetings lined up for today, so hopefully something there will pan out." He didn't mention Stella Bish — Ivy wasn't the only one who could hold information back.

"Oh," Ivy said, "do you have to go right away?"

Dex checked the time at the bottom right of his vision. "I've got a few minutes, why?"

"Well," Ivy said, somehow looking shy and smug at the same time. It suited her. "I asked Renna, Bill and Julie to join us. They doesn't know anything, but I thought this might be a better way for you to meet. If you still want to talk to them, that is."

Ivy must be paranoid about her friends finding out about Reuben if she felt compelled to orchestrate a meeting herself.

"Will they be here soon?" Dex asked.

"Any minute now," Ivy said and Dex nodded. They sat in silence for a while, when Ivy's face focussed on a space behind Dex. He turned and saw a fairly ordinary-looking female avatar link in. She had short red hair and wore a matching red pantsuit. Nothing about her glinted off of anything.

"Renna, hey, over here." Ivy stood, smiling and the other woman walked toward the table. Dex stood and dipping his head in a polite nod, said hello. As they were about to sit, two more people walked in — a tall, well built man with gold skin and an equally tall, thin woman with an almost transparent pair of wings growing out of her back.

"Hey, Ivy," the woman said, "hi, Renna." She looked at Dex, a quizzical expression on her face.

"I didn't know we were having company," the man said, a smile on his face. He turned to face Dex. "I'm Bill and this," he put his hand on the thin woman's shoulder, "is Julie." They sat and Ivy introduced Dex. "This is Andersson Dexter, an investigator." She imbued the word with a campy feel, as if he were an cowboy or a vid actor.

"And what are you investigating, Mr. Dexter?" Renna had a soft, inquisitive voice.

Ivy opened her mouth as if to answer for him, but he said, "There's always something to figure out around here. Right now I'm working on the case of a multiple identity which was erased without its creator's consent." He looked evenly at Renna. Her face displayed nothing that Dex could read, but Ivy's eyes got big and she quickly forced a smile.

"Mr. Dexter was inquiring at work about some technical details and he was referred to me. While we were talking he mentioned this place." Ivy gestured at the bar and turned to her friends. "The way he described it, I thought you all would like it and look who's here? Isn't that funny?"

Dex rolled his eyes, glad that his avatar didn't mimic his bodily reactions. The coincidence was believable enough, but the delivery of the line was something else. The three of them seemed to buy it well enough, though.

"Well, it was his recommendation, now, wasn't it?" Julie said, chiding Ivy slightly in the way old friends do. "It's not that odd that he's here." She smiled at him warmly.

"And it's a good thing, too," Bill said, "so we can thank him. This place is great." He smiled broadly and looked around the bar. Dex flinched inwardly, hoping the four of them weren't about to become regulars at what he thought of as his real office.

"It suits me," he said, simply.

"It certainly does," Renna said, her smile wide. "You don't see too many real gentlemen these days."

Dex took it as a cue and stood up. He picked his hat up off the table and holding it lightly in his hand, said, "And a shame that is. Now, ladies," he nodded at Ivy, Renna and Julie, then turned to face the man. "Bill, I'm afraid that it's time for me to be moving on. Things to investigate and all that." He smiled, doffed his hat and linked out of Monte's.

# EIGHT

DEX WAS TO meet Stella Bish in a trendy section of Marionette City, in an "open air market". He didn't really get the concept of open air in a virtual world, but he supposed it was just another place for avatars to meet or try and sell their digital crap. He linked in to the market and set about looking for Bish. He was just on time and didn't know his way around, so checked the map to see if she was in the area. His map overlay showed her at a bench in the northeast quadrant and he linked over to the area. As his avatar materialized, he recognized her. Once he could move, he walked over to the bench and stood in front of her.

"I'm Andersson Dexter," he said, touching the brim of his hat.

"Yes, I see that," Bish said, referring to the setting that shows printed names hovered over each avatar. Dex had that setting turned off usually; he found it more distracting than useful.

"May I?" He indicated the seat next to her on the bench and she nodded. Dex sat and waited a moment. "You knew Reuben Cobalt?"

"Yes," Bish answered, looking ahead. "He did some work for me." An avatar for Marionette City, Dex wondered. Was Bish a multi?

"If I might ask, what kind of work was that?"

She turned to face Dex, her left knee very nearly touching his right. "What kind of investigator are you, exactly?" she asked.

"The kind who asks the questions," he answered, holding her gaze, "not answers them."

"I see," she said, turning back to look out over the market.

"Have you ever wished that things were different, Mr. Dexter?"

It was a strange question, out of the blue, but Dex figured he should follow her line of thinking, so answered. "Sure. My line of work, all I ever see is things that shouldn't be the way they are. Of course I've wished things were different. Why?"

"I don't mean changing history, Mr. Dexter, though there's a place for that, too, in a manner of speaking. No, I mean the little things — how you open your mail, how you get into your apartment, what noise your system makes to wake you in the morning. The little things, Mr. Dexter," she turned to face him again, "that makes life what it is."

Dex didn't know what to say, so he did what he always did in situations like that — he kept his mouth shut. She looked at him intently for a half minute, then sat back. "I'm what you might call an arranger," she said. "I can arrange for things to be the way you want them to be. It's perfectly legal, mostly and it just comes with a price. Of course, I need people to make the things my clients desire. That's where Reuben came in. Such a talent," she sighed, her gaze taking on a far-away look. "I almost believe that man could do anything — I think if he put his mind to it he could make an entire system mind-activated. He was genius with interfaces. Incredible."

"You brokered Reuben's avatar business?" Dex asked.

"Avatars?" Bish said, derisively. "Hardly. He was too good for that kind of gross graphics work. No, I used Reuben for the complex stuff — recreating ancient interfaces for people, making systems respond to neural cues, occasionally circumventing the artificial barriers to a full experience of the 'nets." She looked at Dex sidelong, as if to check if he was calling Security right now. He wasn't.

"How long had Reuben been working for you?" he asked.

"About a year," she answered. "It's not a full time gig, you know. Just contracts here and there. The money is quite competitive but to be perfectly honest I do believe that he likes — that he liked the challenge more than the compensation."

Dex wondered. Ivy had never mentioned working for Bish and he was sure that even her swiss cheese natural memory would have retained a second employer. He thanked Bish for her time and stood. She remained seated on the bench, looking up at him through surprisingly thick eyelashes. "Let me give you my card," she said, her voice low and dripping with sensuality. She pinged his system and as he accepted, her contact information flowed into his database and the image of a small card appeared in his avatar's hand.

"If there's ever something you want," she said, standing up, her avatar nearly touching his, "something special, unique," she leaned in so that her lips were almost brushing his ear and whispered, "you call me." She paused and Dex felt his physical body flush. It was a most disconcerting feeling and he was relieved when she linked away, the avatar fading to invisibility before him.

● ● ●

Dex unfocussed and got up from his chair. He went into the lav and splashed some water on his face. He refilled his glass from the bottle on the table, swirling the content around. He made a note to pick up another bottle on the way home from work the next day. He stretched and sat down again. He had about an hour to kill before his appointment with Tequila Kate. Another man would have taken a three quarter hour hit of SleepingJuice, played a game or hired a hooker. Dex paged over to his video collection and loaded a file.

This time Dex picked a later video, one he'd watched more times that he wished to admit. He watched his younger self help his friend Maksym pack and watched them both drink, Maks getting drunker as the night wore on, Dex remembering how for once it was like drinking water, the numbness he felt keeping him sober. He skipped through the video, stopping at particular songs, or the looks on Maksym's face, or that one moment as he was refilling their glasses when he nearly said something, nearly asked Maks why, how had things changed, how could he fix it. Dex finished his drink, stopping the image as Maks stood in the doorway, his face inscrutable. Some days Dex liked to imagine it was a look of regret, but this night he just closed his eyes for a moment and ended the file.

● ● ●

Dex followed the link Tequila Kate had sent him and found himself stuck in between worlds for a moment. The link was not to a bar, café or market as he'd assumed. Rather it was to a privately owned location and his identity was being checked against a guest list of sorts. The process didn't take a long time, but it was still an uncomfortable experience. Dex successfully linked in and found himself in a small open space with some couches, chairs, even a lecture area. There were a half dozen other avatars there, chatting amongst themselves and Dex could see some video and text screens which were set up as well to accommodate people who were not accessing the area by avatar.

He looked for Tequila Kate and soon discovered that she was the flamboyantly attired avatar with a literally flaming hairdo that swirled above, around and behind her as she moved. He pinged her and she stood to greet him. She moved toward him and they found a pair of seats out of the way of the other people.

"So, you're an independent investigator," she said, looking Dex up and down.

"And you're a multi rights activist," he countered.

"Well, I'm glad to see we know who we are," she said, grinning and settled in to the seat. "You're investigating Reuben Cobalt's murder."

"Yes."

"And you're calling it a murder?" She arched an eyebrow as she asked the question.

Dex didn't rise to her bait. "Yes." He didn't see any reason to get into a political discussion this early on in the conversation and he figured it was his turn for questions anyway. "How long have you known Reuben?"

"A few years," she answered. "He became active in the community a few years ago. His first — that's what we call the person who creates an alternate identity — his first was worried about being outed, which is a real concern for us. There are plenty of people out there who would never refer to the death of a multi as murder. They'd think of it as cleaning up."

"I'm aware of the, ah, various opinions," Dex said. "But I'm mostly interested in Reuben. Had he received any threats specifically? Was there anyone who had it in for him personally?"

Kate shook her head. "I don't know," she said. "He never mentioned anything like that. When I first got to know him, it was though our support boards. That's how most of the new people come in — looking for a safe place to talk about their experiences. But Reuben soon grew to be more of a resource. And of course, there was his great gift to the community." She gestured around her.

"Avatars," Dex said and Kate nodded.

"When I started, I spent an obscene amount on mine," she said, "and it was a much more complex process for me to log in than it is now, thanks to Reuben. His program was gold to us."

"It was a business for him, though, wasn't it?"

"Sure," Kate said, "but he didn't gouge anyone. It was entirely reasonable. In fact, there are plenty of designers out there who ask more than he did and that's just for the body. What Reuben offered was a chance at a normal life, for the price of a nice outfit." She fixed Dex with a steely gaze. "He was a champion in this community."

"Anyone disagree with that assessment?" Dex asked.

"Well," she said, "you'd have to assume that those people who are trying to root us out of society weren't going to be in love with anyone who was making it easier for multis to fit in."

"How would they know?" Dex asked. "Your community is closed and moderated."

"You got in," she said, "didn't you?" Dex smiled ruefully. "We have security measures," she continued, "but nothing is foolproof. We get our share of griefers and worse. Let me introduce you to someone." She stood and walked over to the main group. She came back with a nondescript fellow, who introduced himself as Jacob Sherman.

"Jacob is our security guy," Kate said, with a grin. "His first is, ah, in your line of work, I think." She smiled at the two men, then turned. "I'll let you two talk shop for awhile. Later." She walked back to the main group and Dex turned to face Sherman.

"This is kind of weird for me," Sherman said, refusing to meet Dex's gaze. "Would you be okay with linking over to Monte's?" Dex was taken aback at the suggestion, but agreed. He linked over and as the bar materialized around him, he wondered what was up with the change of scenery. He made a bee line for his usual table to wait for Sherman, when he caught sight of Jay Shiraishi materializing. Shiraishi had been on the goon squad with Dex when he'd started and was looking to be a lifer on the squad. He was in line to lead the team after Pat Malone moved on.

Dex waved and was about to let his old buddy know that he was on the job when Shiraishi pinged him, saying, "Thanks for coming. I figured it would be easier to talk, here," he gestured at the bar, then at his own avatar, "like this."

# NINE

DEX ORDERED A drink and for a change got it with the neural stimulator response active. It cost more than just drinking the real booze he had sitting in front of him at home, but Dex wasn't prepared to divide his attention between this conversation and his physical surroundings and he needed a drink to go with this chat. "Goddamn it, Shiraishi, were you planning on getting around to talking to me anytime soon?" Dex was trying to keep his voice level.

"I didn't know, man," Shiraishi answered, bringing his own pint of lager to his lips. "I don't usually read the Ds files and it didn't come up at squad. At least, no one mentioned his name. I really didn't know until TK told me."

"Shit," Dex said, sighing. "Well, you're here now. Spill it, Jay. How well did you know the vic?"

"He did my avatar for me," Shiraishi said. "The other one, I mean. I knew him to say hello to. I've seen him around the compound — that's what they call the joint where we just were. Other than that, nothing. We weren't buddies or anything like that. Besides, he's busy with the avatars and I'm busy with Security. There wasn't a whole lot of socializing for either of us at TK's events."

"Fine." Dex tipped his glass back and felt the unfamiliar rush of simulated drunkenness mixing with the real thing. "What can you tell me, then?"

"How much experience have you had with multis?" Shiraishi asked, sipping his own drink. Dex refilled his glass, but had the invisible bartender hold the effects this time.

"Honestly, not a lot," he answered. "As far as I know, this is my first case. I mean, I know there are multis out there and I've never given a good god damn one way or another about it, but that's where it starts and ends."

"Fair enough," Shiraishi said. "It's a complicated thing. On the one hand, there's a long history of people having multiple identities. Back before the everywherenet, most people did, whether they wanted to or not. It was so common that there were entire businesses built out of helping people consolidate all their identities into a cohesive unit. Of course, once the firms got together and made the everywherenet happen, everyone had to pick a single identity and stick with it if they wanted access. And once online access became integrated with personal systems, that identity was pretty much chosen for you."

"But people still have separate identities for boards, games, sex, the usual stuff."

"Sure," Shiraishi agreed, "but those are really just pseudonyms. If push comes to shove, the everywherenet knows it's you."

Dex thought for a moment. "Which means that anyone can figure out who that hot little number is," he cocked his head toward an obvious prostitute on one of the bar stools, "if they really want to bad enough."

"Exactly," Shiraishi said. "And, of course, there are the logs. We all know that logs are kept of all our activities somewhere in the bowels of everywherenet's data storage and we all know they're erased after a couple of weeks. But they're there, so there's no way to really ever hide what you do. If you do something bad enough and someone with money or pull cares enough, soon enough, you'll get caught. It's that simple. So a true multi, an identity like kind that Reuben helped people create, it's what everyone fears and desires. Real anonymity. The chance to hide or the chance to change yourself." He sat back in his chair and lifted his glass in a toast. "Freedom."

"Okay, so there's more to multiple identities that meets the eye," Dex said, "I can accept that. But what's up with all the Security? Is it really that dangerous and if it is, how come there aren't stories like Reuben's all the time?"

"Well, I'll admit there's a healthy dose of paranoia within the community," Shiraishi said, "but that's partly because there really are admins whose job it is to hunt down and eliminate multis in a firm's internal system..."

"That's different," Dex broke in, "they're protecting the integrity of their system. Not the same thing at all."

"Fine," Shiraishi said, "but what's to stop those same firms from getting those same admins to do that same job on the public everywherenet?"

"Oh for chrissakes, Shiraishi," Dex said, putting his glass down on the table hard, "you've been eating your own dog food so long you think it's filet mignon. Just because they could do that, it doesn't mean they would. I mean, hell's bells, the firms can barely get together enough to run the everywherenet, you really think they're going to donate resources to fund a manhunt for multis? Please."

"Do you really think it's that unlikely?" Shiraishi said, sounding a little put out. "The firms made damn sure that the everywherenet knows exactly who's doing what and where. And it's not just online activity, either." He looked at Dex knowingly.

"Okay," Dex said, "we know the logs show both online and physical activity. So?"

"So they want the info, man," Shiraishi said, exasperated. "If they want it, they're going to want it for everyone. And that means no one slipping through the cracks. No multis."

"I don't know," Dex said. "That's pretty weak."

"You don't have to believe it," Shiraishi said, "but you asked and I'm telling you. And there definitely are individuals who are hunting down multis, whether they're on a clock or not."

"What do you mean?"

"People get harassed and people get deleted. Usually it's not multis who are so far into the scene that they have avatars, but yeah, people do just disappear."

"Are we talking technical erasure," Dex asked, "or old fashioned intimidation?"

"It's a bit of both," Shiraishi said, "usually intimidation. There are a few renegade admin types who troll the boards looking for multis, crack the authentication and delete the accounts. Nothing we can even do about that, except help people revive the identity. Also, they usually have to go board by board to do that — it's more of a nuisance than anything. To be fair, working Security for the compound the major concern is anonymity for the firsts and keeping the looky-lous out."

"Ever investigated a murder?" Dex asked, flat out.

"No," Shiraishi answered, meeting his old comrade's gaze. "Though we'd likely never have known about it anyway. When people disappear, that's the point. They're gone."

Dex paused. He pulled up the image of Reuben that Ivy had sent him and sent it to Shiraishi. "This one didn't disappear." Dex watched as Shiraishi's avatar's face stopped changing. He wondered what the man's true reaction was to the image.

When he finally spoke, Shiraishi's voice was soft. "Fuck, Dex, what did they do to him?"

"Reprogrammed him into a loop. His, whatever you call it, first, didn't even know it was happening."

"Whoa," Shiraishi said, "this is some heavy shit. If we've got a multi-hating programmer on the loose with these kind of skills... I'd better warn TK." Shiraishi made to get up, but Dex put out a hand to stop the man.

"Slow down, big fella," Dex said. "As far as we know, this is a one-off. There's no indication that this is an anti-multi crime. Odds are it's a personal thing; murder usually is. Don't go off all half-cocked and scare the crap out of your little community." Shiraishi sat back down and rubbed his face with his hands.

"But what if there is some sick fuck out there with a hard-on for multis and a bag of evil code? What if this happens to someone else?" It was a good question, one Dex couldn't really answer.

"I don't know," Dex conceded, "but what good is scaring everyone going to do? We don't know who it is, or how the reprogramming happened. We don't even have any leads to tell people to watch out for this or for that. All we have is something to fear, just problems without solutions. And what's the point of that?"

The men were quiet, the sounds of the bar's music playing over each one's thoughts. Shiraishi stood and broke the silence. "I'll give you two days. If you can't give me a reason not to by then, I'm posting this to the community. Image and all." He linked out of the bar without another word and Dex shook his head.

The last thing he needed was Shiraishi running around giving all the multis on the 'nets nightmares. Even if there were a serial multi killer out there, which Dex had no reason to believe, all a full scale panic would do is tip that person off to who the multis were. It was a dumb, rookie move, but Dex understood. They were his people. He was one of them, they were his community and he wanted to protect them. Dex understood, but he didn't share those feelings. After all, he had no one to protect.

He linked out of Marionette City and looked around his tiny apartment. The kind of real world jobs he took, this was the best sort of thing he could expect. Of course, with his Cubicle Men salary, he could have afforded a private place, but why bother. He didn't need any more space; he didn't have any things to put in it. He spent his extra money on disk upgrades, music files and once in a while on something with a little more class than Jamaica's Best.

He hit the lav and drank some water, trying to get the non-taste of virtual booze out of his mouth. He doused the lights with a thought and took a swig of SleepingJuice. His last thought was extinguished before it could even be fully formed.

# TEN

AFTER HIS TYPICAL gulp of Flying Fish, five minutes in the lav, dressed and out the door routine, Dex fired up his system on the train ride in to B&B and sent off a message to Alvaro Zuccarelli. No more Mr. Nice Guy, it was time to start getting answers. By the time he was getting his first mug of coffee flavoured sludge, he had a meeting set up in Marionette City with Zuccarelli. The banker held offices there and Dex had been forced to make an appointment. Fine, they could play it Zuccarelli's way; Dex didn't mind so long as he got what he wanted out of the man.

He was part way through the third call of the morning when his internal system interrupted with an emergency message. He put the B&B customer on hold and checked it out. Someone was calling him on the emergency channel, sending nothing but a link to Marionette City. The Cubicle Men's emergency system had access to that channel, as well as the automated everywherenet channel for disaster warnings or public health scares, but that was it. He had never had this happen before, so he just went straight in to see what was going on. As the linked area was materializing around him, he could see a humanoid form already there, waiting.

It took a couple of seconds to fully log into Marionette City, which was good news for Dex. He was just beginning to make out the form in the blocky world forming in his vision, when he saw what appeared to be a small explosion emanating from the middle of the shape in front of him. His instincts from his years in the goon squad kicked in and he hard aborted the login. As he was killing the process, he sent an urgent message to Annabelle. She responded immediately by voice.

"What's up Dex?" she said, a hint of surprise in her voice. "Is this business or pleasure?"

Dex couldn't be bothered with the niceties. "I think someone is trying to kill me," he said, "in Marionette City."

"What?" she asked incredulously and Dex briefly explained what he'd seen in the second or so before he killed the login procedure.

"I'm going in," Annabelle said, "send me a link." Dex did as she asked, then asked her to send him real time visuals of what she saw. She agreed and linked in to his last position.

She logged in and Dex saw the same images he'd seen just seconds before, only without the other form nearby. Annabelle turned on her heads up display, looking for nearby activity — there were a few avatars hanging out in that location, but nothing stood out as strange. "Damn it!" Dex said, "he's gone."

"Not so fast, mister," Annabelle said, bringing up an unfamiliar screen on her display. "I've got a few tricks up my sleeve, you know." She entered some commands and the world around her seemed to shimmer. "And they say time travel is impossible," she said, as Dex saw the space around him change.

"What the hell?"

"I've got a backdoor patch into the master log," Annabelle said. "We can't change anything, but we can see what happened. So, let's go back, say, two minutes?"

"Sounds about right," Dex said, amazed. His viewer looked like it was showing a vid running in reverse, avatars coming and going and at one point he saw the flash. "There it is," he said.

"Let's go back a bit further and see what we get," Annabelle said as the images continued to run back. The shape Dex saw when the explosion happened left the area and Annabelle stopped the rewind. Dex saw an avatar enter the area, dressed in the most basic outfit available, the default avatar when someone first activates an account in Marionette City. It was blank looking in every way, performing no gestures of any kind, the face and body entirely neutral. The only thing about it that differentiated it from a completely newborn avatar was that it was holding something. Something that looked like a handgun.

Dex saw himself beginning to materialize and the avatar lifted the weapon, aiming it at a badly pixellated version of Dex's avatar. He saw the gun fire and saw his own avatar link out of Marionette City at the same time. The gunman stood still for a moment, continuing to aim the weapon, then disappeared.

"Any idea who that was?" Dex asked. "Or what he was trying to do?"

Annabelle was quiet for a while, as text and images scrolled over her display. "I think I'm getting something," she said. "Hang on, I have to link out. I'll call you back in a sec."

The images in front of Dex's vision disappeared and he noticed the blinking light in his peripheral vision, indicating that he had a B&B client still on hold. He quickly reviewed the recorded client call, refreshing his memory. The poor sap was trying to cancel his support account and Dex was following the company line of trying to keep the customer on the books as long as possible. Fuck it, he didn't have time for this. Dex picked up the call and before the customer could start screaming at him, he nicely said, "There we go, your account is canceled and a refund for the last month is on its way. Thank you for choosing Barrett and Brar," and he ended the call. A few finger waves and everything he had said became true. He'd catch hell for it at the monthly meeting, but he had bigger fish to fry.

Annabelle had been pinging him as he was finishing the B&B call and he answered her as soon as he could. "Bad news, Dex," she said. "It was a bot."

"A bot?"

"Yeah," she sighed, "a script someone wrote up to create a throwaway avatar who was trying to infect your account with a virus."

"What?" Dex asked, perplexed. "What the hell is that supposed to do? Everlock would just kill it before it even got in. Who cares?"

Everlock was the pervasive anti-malware program that filled everywherenet and made it safe to plug the implanted human/silicon hybrid computer system everyone used straight into the public 'nets. Annabelle explained. "Everlock will kill the virus, sure, and you'd be just fine. But as a consequence of it finding the virus, you'd be locked out of Marionette City for a while. Maybe even a day or more, while Everlock pulled out the destructive code."

"So the bot wasn't actually trying to kill me," Dex said, "just slow me down."

"Looks that way," Annabelle said. "Though there's a few interesting things in here. You didn't actually get a full hit of the virus, so you're good to go. I did manage to get it all copied to my own system and I'm reading the source now. It looks like your friendly neighborhood killbot is lazy."

"What do you mean?"

"It looks like he just recycled the code he'd used before," she said, "I'm pretty sure this is the code that did the number on your vic."

"What the fuck?" Dex said, his jaw open.

"Well, I've been thinking about this one," Annabelle said, "I, ah, took the liberty of downloading your case file and reading it over. Hope you don't mind."

"That's fine," Dex said, impatiently, "that's what it's for. What do you think?"

"Well, your vic was a lot like this bot — just a virtual construction within Marionette City, built to emulate an individual login, but separate. It's complicated to do, certainly more complicated for your vic than the bot, but it's just code in the end. What makes Everlock work is that we're not just code. There are built in protections in the interface between the wetware and the silicon, hardware protections. You'd never notice it, but there's a very slight lag between anything passing the barrier between the hardware and wetware and that's where Everlock does its magic. But for a construct that's pure code, that barrier doesn't exist. They're still vulnerable to malware and that's what this is."

"So you're saying that Reuben was killed by a virus?"

"Well, technically, no," Annabelle said. "There's no indication here that the code is designed to self-replicate. But it was foreign malware introduced into the system." She added, coldly, "And, of course, you can't kill something that's not real."

Dex ignored her last comment. "And what would it have done to me if I had been infected?" Dex asked.

"Actually, this is the interesting thing," Annabelle said, warming up to the subject again, "it actually wouldn't have done anything. It would have just failed to run. The bot really wasn't intended to hurt you, assuming its writer knew anything about the code it was deploying. All it would do is trigger the Everlock login freeze."

Dex leaned back in his chair and thought. "Can you trace the bot?" he asked. "See who wrote it, who's controlling it?"

"Dunno," Annabelle said, "I can try." She paused. "But it'll cost you."

"What," Dex said, annoyed, "what do you mean?"

"Dinner," she said. "Take me out to dinner tonight and I'll see what I can find for you."

"I... but..." Dex sputtered.

"Good," Annabelle said. "I'll make a reservation and send you the link. 'Til tonight, then." She ended the call and Dex sighed. People, he thought. Can't live with 'em.

• • •

Dex had to scramble to keep his appointment with Zuccarelli. He linked in to Marionette City directly to the building where the banker kept his offices. Dex checked the directory and found the rooms where he was to meet Zuccarelli. He walked through the construct, wondering how much effort it had taken to reproduce a historical four storey brick walk up and why anyone would bother. He climbed the stairs for two floors and halfway down the hall came to a door with Zuccarelli's name stenciled on the faux glass.

Dex knocked and the door opened. Alvaro Zuccarelli was seated behind an enormous slate desk with nothing on it, not moving, seeming to stare off into space. It was a disconcerting image, but Dex simply walked up to the desk, put his palms flat on its surface and leaned in toward the other man.

"Enough bullshit," he said, looking Zuccarelli in the eyes. "I have had a very bad couple of hours and you do not want to make me an enemy today. Reuben Cobalt. Tell me everything you know."

Zuccarelli smiled, as if he were accustomed to being threatened. "I'm sure a man in your position can appreciate the value of discretion, Mr. Dexter. My clients do expect certain... additional benefits with their accounts here."

"Can it with the sales pitch," Dex said, sitting in the chair opposite the desk. "I'm not in the market. Reuben Cobalt is dead."

"What?" Zuccarelli's smile disappeared. "How is that possible?"

"It appears that he was murdered," Dex answered, coldly.

"Murdered?" Zuccarelli looked genuinely shocked, but a man of his means would have an avatar that could fake anything. "Poor Ivy," he said, softly.

"Do you know what her connection to Reuben Cobalt was?" Dex asked.

Zuccarelli looked at Dex in the eye. "She never made that clear to me and it was not my place to ask. One needs to be open minded in my business, Mr. Dexter."

"Fine," Dex said. "Then open your mind about Reuben Cobalt and tell me everything you know."

"Very well," Zuccarelli said. "I was Reuben Cobalt's banker. That's all. It wasn't even a terribly interesting account. At first it was just small transfers in from Ivy's account, but then Reuben started to get work of his own and I was more involved. What do you want — copies of his records?"

"Yes," Dex said, "that would be a good start."

"Fine," Zuccarelli sighed and pinged Dex's system. He accepted the download and a small spreadsheet appeared in his inbox. "What else?"

"What else have you got?" Dex asked, reminded of his old goon squad days. Sometimes it was fun to intimidate the witnesses.

"Nothing, really," Zuccarelli said. "I didn't know him well and honestly I have a program that handles most of the day to day affairs."

Dex was scanning through Reuben's records and whistled under his voice when he saw the final account balance. "He had a tidy bundle in here," Dex said, "even after your usurious take." Zuccarelli sniffed. "So, what's going to happen to it?"

"Given the situation," Zuccarelli said, "I'll be transferring it to Ivy's account. Seems appropriate."

"Indeed," Dex agreed. "So," he said, switching tacks, "how do you know Ivy?"

Zuccarelli hesitated, as if deciding whether a lie would be preferable to the truth. He seemed to get a resigned look on his face and Dex figured that he'd be getting at least some version of the truth. "She built this place for me," he gestured at the space around him.

"The room, or..."

"No, the building," Zuccarelli said. "I own the whole thing."

"I see," Dex said, "you hired her firm?"

"No," Zuccarelli said, "she was moonlighting for me. Through... my other life I became aware of her work at her firm. I think it was her first time as an independent — I paid her with cash and my services. She still has a small account with me. Now that Reuben is gone... well, I suppose I'll see more of her now."

"Guess so," Dex said. He stood and thanked Zuccarelli for his time. "I might very well be back," he said, before leaving. "And if you think of anything that might be useful..."

"I'll be in touch, of course," Zuccarelli said and Dex linked out of the man's office. He had to go put on his date tie.

# ELEVEN

DEX DIDN'T HAVE time to go shopping for a new tie, let alone a new suit. It had been a while since he'd been hoodwinked into taking someone to dinner and his good tie was, he realized now, hideously ugly. He put it on anyway and changed his view so that he could get a good look at his avatar. The suit his avatar always wore was fine and he'd always been fond of the hat. But the tie — what had he ever been thinking? Bright red and shiny against his charcoal suit. Ugh. It wasn't that ugly, he told himself, so long as you just closed your eyes and didn't look at it. Whatever. It was only Annabelle and it was under duress. Maybe she'd take the tie as a hint.

By now Dex was physically back at his apartment and he took a minute to unfocus from Marionette City and make his body comfortable. He changed clothes, used the lav and poured the last of the Jamaica's Best into a tumbler. He hadn't had time to get another bottle, so he would have to drink the virtual crap. At least he could get a glass of the real stuff in now.

He settled into his comfortable chair and went back online. At least the restaurant Annabelle had picked wasn't one of those million dollar places that would cost Dex a week's pay. He linked over a minute or two early and got to the table first. He flipped through the menu and tried to remember the last time he'd even been to a restaurant. He just didn't understand the point of tasting food but not getting full. Still, if Annabelle had anything useful for him, it would be worth it. So long as he didn't think about the tie.

Annabelle arrived precisely on time and she had definitely put more effort into this than Dex had. She had done something to her chin length hair, made it all pouffy and sparkly and she wore a dress. Dex didn't think he'd ever seen her in dress before — he always thought she was strictly a utilitarian dresser. But this night she had on some kind of semi transparent thing with a slight purple glow to it. Underneath she wore a couple of tiny bands of strategically placed purple fabric. Shit. This could get complicated.

"Hey, Dex," she said as she sat down across from him. "Looking good." Dex rolled his eyes and cursed his tie.

"Yeah," he answered, "you, too." They each looked at the menu and placed their orders with the table's service screen. Their glasses filled immediately and Dex took a long swallow of the fake dark and stormy. It wasn't that bad after all. "So, got anything for me?" he asked. Annabelle arched an eyebrow, grinning and he hastened to add, "From the code you took earlier."

Her smile faltered and she said, "Yeah, the code. Well, there's good news and bad news. The good news is that I'm ninety nine percent sure that we don't have a a multi-hating serial killer on our hands. The code that got your vic was specifically non-replicating. It was made for him and him alone."

"Well, that's good to know," Dex said, beginning to compose a message to Jay Shiraishi while they talked. "And the bad news?"

"Bad news is that's all I know," Annabelle looked away from his gaze. "There's nothing there to identify where it came from. The code itself is just stand-alone malware — there's nothing that identifies it at all. And the bot was very carefully made, not tied to another system, at least not that I can see." She caught his eyes and looked away again. "I mean, there has to be a real system running the damn thing, but I just can't get back to it. They did a good job Dex. It was the real deal."

"Strange," he said, thinking. "From what I've heard, Reuben was the best in the business for that sort of thing. And it seems unlikely that he killed himself, since Ivy is the one who hired me. Besides, he... or she would have had so many easier ways to do it. What would be the point?"

"Beats me," Annabelle said. At that moment, the first course arrived. Dex could smell Annabelle's escargot and it just made him hungry. He picked a piece of what was supposed to be some kind of smoked fish out of his salad and tasted it. The flavour in his mouth was strong, but it just wasn't the same as eating. He'd have been happier with a food brick, but Annabelle seemed to be enjoying herself.

"So," Dex said, when the table had appeared to swallow their empty appetizer plates, "you do this sort of thing often?"

"Eating?" Annabelle asked, looking confused.

"Yeah," Dex said, leaning back a bit. "You know, going to restaurants, blackmailing people into coming with you; the whole dating thing."

"Ah," she said. "I guess. I mean, I've been out a few times — it's something to do. Everyone does, right? We're all looking for that someone."

"I don't know if we all do," Dex said, "and I don't think there is a someone."

"Sure there is," she smiled at him and leaned in. "There's someone out there for everyone — even if you need a pickaxe, a compass, and night goggles to find them." She laughed and Dex found himself grinning in spite of himself.

"Maybe for you," he said, "but some of us are just better off alone." At that moment, their meals arrived and they spent a few awkward moments with the food. When the table cleared their plates. Dex began, "Look, I'm sorry..."

"Don't be," Annabelle interrupted him, "I'm not looking for a lifetime here. Why don't we just have a night together — I'm free, you're free. Nothing intimate, just sex."

"Just sex?"

"You know," she said, laughing, "enjoyable act between two creatures in a species in response to biological and neurological stimuli?"

"Yeah," Dex said, smiling sadly. "I know what it is. I just... well, it's not you, I just..."

"What?" she said, softly.

"I, ah," Dex tried to find a delicate way to put his thoughts. "I have a different preference."

"Oh," she said, eyebrows lifting. "That doesn't have to be a problem. I'm no prude." Her body shimmered slightly and then turned slowly and surprisingly seamlessly into someone else. Her hair shortened to an above the ear short cut, the dress condensed into a pair of fitted trousers and a t-shirt and the underneath bands changed as well. The top band disappeared entirely, revealing a very solid set of male pectoral muscles and the bottom bands formed into underpants sporting a substantial and prominent package. "Do you like this better?"

Dex had nothing to say and Annabelle said, "I don't mind dressing up occasionally. Whatever works for you."

"No," he finally got out, "that's exactly the problem. I don't enjoy any of this."

"You don't like sex?"

"Not like this," he said, gesturing around them. "If there isn't touching, real body touching, I just... I just don't like it." Dex felt his face get hot and wondered if he could get away with just linking out of the restaurant. Instead, they sat together in silence for a moment. "It's not you," he said, finally. "You're... great. Either way. If I met you on the train or something, well, who knows, right? But..."

"It's okay," she said, the avatar standing up, shimmering and turning back to Annabelle, the girl. "If it doesn't work, it doesn't work," she said, a little sadly but with genuine feeling, "I do understand." Dex stood and walked toward her. He kissed her lightly on the cheek and she smiled. "Thanks," she said. "It might not do anything for you, but that was nice for me."

"Thanks for your help on the case," he said, then immediately hated himself for sounding like such a heel. Annabelle smiled, though.

"Anytime," she said. "You know if you ever change your mind..."

"If I do, you'll be the first one I call," he said, smiling. He waited for her to link out of the restaurant, then checked to make sure she was offline before he linked over to Monte's.

• • •

"Why the long face?" the bartender said and Dex knew better than to search the bot's face for any hint of humour. There wasn't any.

"It's been a rough day," Dex said, accepting the double dark and stormy with extra neural stims. He took a sip and felt the strange rush of the false liquor hit his system.

"You wanna talk about it?" the bartender asked, as it always did, as it was programmed to do.

"No," Dex said and the bar bot turned and walked down to the other end of the bar, unoffended. He took another sip of his drink and looked at his reflection in the mirror behind the bar. Not bad for a guy who didn't give a damn, he thought, tie or no tie. He knew he didn't see what Annabelle saw and wondered if he should have just gone with her. He probably could have faked it for an hour or two; it would have made her happy, if only for the moment. But he knew he couldn't keep it up, the charade, pretending he felt something when he never did.

It was bad enough sitting here, in this fake bar, drinking fake booze served by a fake bartender. Just because he wanted that feeling, the one you get sitting alone in a crowded room, somehow more solitary than if you really were alone. Though, of course, the funny reality of it all was that Dex was actually alone, in his apartment, staring off into space. There were just so many levels of deception in the modern world. He didn't think he was cut out for it. This new world. Born too late, that's what Maks used to say, they were a couple of guys who were just born at the wrong time in history.

But Maks figured it out, somehow. How to fit in, make it all make some kind of sense. He'd figured it out, but never filled Dex in on the secret. He just walked out the door, out of Dex's life and he'd taken the secret with him. Dex took a long pull on his drink and wondered, not for the first time, what Maks was doing now. He wondered if Maks ever thought of him, of the life they had lived back when they both believed that they could make a place where things could be different.

Where things could be different. Dex fished in his pockets and found the card that Stella Bish had given him. Do you ever wish things could be different, she'd asked him. Only every second of every day. But there was no program that could make the world the way he wanted it to be. Annabelle's time machine didn't work that way. Still, maybe there was something... something she could do for him to dull the ache. Dull it more than the booze did.

He pulled up his messenger and started to carefully compose a message. After half an hour, he had it ready and sent it off to Bish. Another dark and stormy went by, the bartender now offering sobering tablets along with the drinks. Dex passed, wanting to feel the sweet oblivion and the promised pain the next day. Feeling things — it took a lot in this world to make him feel things.

He was debating on a third drink when his messenger pinged. Bish had a name for him. Uri Farone. He dealt in memories, making them better, making them the way they ought to be. There was no changing the past, but Farone knew how to make it seem as though the past were different. Dex figured that this was the closest he would ever get. He paged over to Farone's board and looked at the satisfied customer testimonials and the various options available for purchase.

It was impressive. According to his PR page, the deluxe package could completely erase the "wrong" memory and replace it with a better one. Of course, the usual caveats applied about not being responsible for any cognitive dissonance created by the process and paradoxes that arose as a result. Dex wondered — if he could fix it so that his memory of Maks was gone, would he be able to live in this world? He focussed back on the bar, its lights flashing, avatars dancing, drinking, fighting and fucking within its false walls. He swallowed the last of his drink and went offline.

Blinking at the seemingly bright lights in his room, Dex stood and worked the kinks out of his body. He shucked off his sweaty clothes and stumbled to the lav. He turned on the shower full blast and found that he had to lean against the side of the tiny room as the water rushed over him. With a lurch, he doubled over and threw up under the shower. Once his stomach settled slightly, he turned off the water, let the blower dry him and the room, then padded out, naked, to fall into bed.

# TWELVE

THE BUZZING IN his head was nearly drowned out by the throbbing. The room was hardly lit at all — the windows had automatically become translucent according to Dex's daily program for the apartment, but the surrounding buildings and cloud cover kept the sunlight a dull dishwater streak. Even so, Dex thought his eyes were going to pop out of his head when he looked toward the weak light. He turned off his system's alarm and at least the buzzing stopped. He felt his gorge rise as soon as he sat up and he grabbed the bottle of Flying Fish on the way to the lav.

After a few minutes on his knees, Dex thought he might be able to keep the tonic down and sipped carefully from the bottle as he turned the shower on quickly to hose down his body and the room. He stayed on the floor as the water turned to warm air and he dried off. He waited a few moments for the electrolytes and other chemicals in the tonic to calm his stomach and sooth the throbbing in his head. He'd get to B&B a few minutes later than usual, but he was already in line for a reprimand for the cancelled account — he figured that another minor infraction didn't really matter much.

Dex yanked his spare uniform out of the autoclave, dressed and grabbed nutrient brick, which he stuffed in his pocket. He took another swig of Flying Fish before he left the apartment and rested his head on the pole of the lift as it spiraled him down to street level. He nibbled gingerly at the food brick as he rode the train to B&B and ended up arriving only a few minutes later than he usually did.

Thankfully, he was on text duty, so he didn't have to actually speak to anyone. He spent the next three hours answering questions ranging from the moronic to the incomprehensible. Aside from the occasional attack of vertigo, it was really the perfect mindset for the job. At break time, Dex grabbed a coffee, then hightailed it back to his work station and called up the contact details for Uri Farone.

Interested customers could get a quote for the "software memory upgrade" of their choice in a variety of ways — there was a text form, a voice messaging line and Farone provided a link to a small kiosk in Marionette City where he or a bot was available 24/7 to help potential clients realize their dreams. The CSR in Dex was impressed with the customer service commitment. He went back to answering client queries, still thinking about Farone's offer.

Dex was self aware enough to know that he had a problem. The disaster of his date with Annabelle only reminded him a truth he had known for a long time. Maybe he wasn't cut out for the modern world, but he was pretty sure there were other people like him, only they didn't spend every spare moment curled up in a bottle watching the same videos of their past on eternal repeat.

Just after he'd first joined up with the Cubicle Men, Dex had actually made an effort to at least pretend to be normal. He'd searched out boards for people who record their lives, ostensibly to hone the technical aspects of the operation, but secretly Dex hoped he might meet someone he could actually talk to. There were plenty of people on the boards that probably would have done, but it never worked out. Dex kept looking for the ease that comes with physical, real world companionship, that connection with another person that he just never felt online. Eventually, he gave up on the boards and just focussed on the work. He told himself there was more than enough stimulation on the job.

And that might even have been true, once. Dex was rarely bored; the work he did as one of the Cubicle Men was fascinating to him and he liked to think he was good at it. He'd certainly been given enough encouragement by his squad leaders. Two full time jobs managed to fill the days and Dex usually didn't feel like he was missing out on anything. But today, this morning, in his stimulant-weakened state, he let himself want things to be different. Maybe Uri Farone's ad text was right — maybe Dex could change the past in order to change the future.

• • •

Dex spent the rest of the day focussed on B&B work; it hurt his head too much to manage two viewers at once. He did send Ivy a message in the afternoon, asking for another meeting. It was time to check in, to find out if she had any other information and see how she reacted to the news that while he hadn't found the killer, he had found the murder weapon. They set an appointment for that evening at Monte's and Dex figured he'd have at least thirty minutes at his apartment before he'd have to link over. On his way back to the apartment, he found himself surprisingly looking forward to the taste of real alcohol. He wondered how he could be in such pain in the morning, but by the time the workday ended, be ready for another drink.

It was raining again, the drops big and cold, making the street slick and drawing up the smell of something long dead from the pavement. The city seemed darker, more ominous to Dex when it rained. It could be just the lack of the weak and ineffective sunlight they usually got, making the world a grimmer place than usual, or maybe it was the shine that made the concrete and metal gleam like a knife in the LED streetlights. Whatever it was, it made Dex's mood even more foul and as he trudged from the train stop to his building, he wished he could skip meeting with Ivy and go straight to bed. Twelve hours of oblivion seemed about right just then. Even so, he stopped in at the store and picked up another bottle of Jamaica's Best to replace the previous day's dead soldier.

Dex spiraled up the lift to his floor, dripping water all the way down the shaft. He stepped off into the dank hallway and walked down the hall and into his apartment. He had his system turn the heat up a couple of degrees as he undressed. He stuffed his wet things along with the previous day's clothes into the autoclave and stepped into the lav. Ten seconds of water, followed by the blower and Dex was almost warm again. He found a light fleece blanket and without bothering with clothes, wrapped himself up. The joys of living alone.

He opened the new bottle of rum and poured a small amount into a mug, then topped it up with ginger ale. He put the mug in the zapper for a half minute, then took his makeshift hot toddy to the chair. He settled in and linked over to Monte's.

He headed for the usual table and ordered a coffee. He was still chilled from the walk and the image of a warm drink fitted his mood better than his usual cocktail. His avatar sipped the coffee while Dex sipped his hot toddy, waiting for Ivy. Dex waited about ten minutes, spending the time catching up on news from around the boards and the Cubicle Men's own feed. He was getting near the end of his coffee when Ivy linked in, looking somewhat frantic.

"What's wrong?" Dex messaged over to her, as she looked for him in the darkened room.

"I'm supposed to be with Renna and the others and I just had a bit of trouble getting away," she said as she walked over to the table. "I don't have very long."

"No problem," Dex said as Ivy sat across from him. "I'll just give you the executive summary. Whoever killed Reuben tried to hit me with the same code."

"Oh my god," Ivy said, her avatar's face registering shock. "Are you okay?"

"Yeah, I'm fine," Dex said. "I linked out before it got me and anyway all it would have done is kept me out of Marionette City for a few days. Everlock would have eaten it."

Ivy nodded gravely and said, "I was always worried about that." Dex looked puzzled and she continued. "The multi avatars. I knew Everlock didn't really do anything for them; I knew they were vulnerable. Oh, Mr. Dexter," Ivy looked panicked. "Is going around? Has it replicated?"

He shook his head. "Don't worry," he said. "That's the other thing. The code was specifically non-replicating. The good news is that means everyone else is okay, or at least they're safe from this. The bad news," he looked in her eyes, "is that someone really specifically didn't like Reuben and I'm no closer to knowing who."

Ivy's avatar's face went slack and she was quiet for a while. "No, that's good news," she said, finally. "I don't know what I did to deserve this, but at least it was only for me. And now that it happened, I can maybe find a way to protect the others from this kind of attack."

Dex was surprised at her reaction, but in all his dealings with the multi community it had been clear that they tended to look out for one another. But there had to be a leak, a crack, a chink in the armour somehow. "Ivy, I need you to tell me something," he said. "The work you do for people in the community, the work Reuben did for Stella Bish, what was all that? Why is it so secret?"

She looked at Dex like an adult looks at a retarded child. "Do you tell everyone you know about this?" she asked, gesturing at the two of them. "Your landlord, your lovers, your regular job, if you have one? Do they all know you live off grid?"

Dex was silent a moment. She had a valid point. "Fair enough," he said, "but what were you doing? Alvaro Zuccarelli told me you started with his building and I know you do avatars for multis, but by the look of Reuben's bank statements, there's a lot more to it than that. What did Reuben do, Ivy?"

"Do you have a regular day job?" she asked. Dex nodded, hoping she'd cut to chase sooner rather than later. "So you're on the two full time job schedule?"

"Sure," he said. "A lot of it is concurrent, if you know what I mean."

"Of course," Ivy said, smiling without warmth. "I've been doing it a while now, myself. I do UI for a big firm for big, normal projects and Reuben does... did UI for Stella Bish, for small, underground projects. I don't know how you do it, but it's been fucking hell for two years. Hardly any time to myself, trying to juggle all the projects, keeping all the secrets... but it all seemed worth it. I was getting somewhere, you know," she said, looking at Dex with sadness in her face. "I thought I was finally getting somewhere."

"I'm not sure I follow you," Dex said, softly.

"I think I just about had it all worked out," she said, talking as much to herself as to Dex. "I think I could have done it."

"Done what?"

"Disappeared," she said, looking up at Dex. "Left Ivy behind once and for all. Become Reuben. Full time, all the time, just Reuben. Who I've always really been all along." Dex was silent, waiting for her to finish. "As soon as I created him, it just felt so much more right. His personality, his body, everything about him... was me. I just never knew it before. I thought..." she paused, as if trying to catch her breath. "I thought I might actually get to be happy."

Dex had nothing to say to that and once he didn't answer her,

Ivy looked embarrassed and begged off to go back to her friends. "They'll come looking for me if I'm away much longer," she said and Dex told her they were done. Ivy linked out of the bar and with no other reason to stay, Dex linked out of Marionette City and went offline. He thought about what she had said and saw the sadness in her face as she remembered how close to happiness she might have been. It was a familiar sight. What remained of his hot toddy had grown cold and Dex threw it down the drain in the middle of the floor in the lav. He drank a glass of water, took a draught of SleepingJuice and slipped into the dark well of sleep.

# THIRTEEN

WHEN DEX AWOKE, the world seemed brighter and generally less horrible than it had for some time. It was amazing what not being critically hung over can do for a man. While he didn't exactly leap from the bed, there was no doubt that he would be out of the apartment and en route to his work station at B&B in the usual amount of time. He might even be a little early, which would hopefully offset the lateness of the previous day.

However, when he arrived at the CSR's room, his messenger immediately went off with an urgent notice to see his manager, Marian. "Aw, fuck," Dex thought. This is going to be annoying and unpleasant. He wasn't sure if he would have to do some serious groveling or if he was just going to get shit-canned right off the bat. It wouldn't be the first time and thanks to some connections within the Cubicle Men, he knew he could get another job without too much hassle. Still, he'd have to change apartments and he'd just gotten used to his current one. He really wasn't excited about the inevitable months of banging into doors in the dark.

Dex dropped his overcoat off at his work station before heading down the hall to the management suite. Why they made him actually physically go to their offices, he'd never understand. It was bad enough that people had to physically be on the premises to do work that only ever occurred over the 'nets anyway. But, that was part of the fun of having a low end job — you got to perform menial tasks and, as a bonus, be used a prop for massaging your boss's ego.

He got to the antechamber of the managers' suite and pinged his boss. The automatic response popped up and told him to wait. As usual. There were no chairs and Dex was left cooling his heels for a good five minutes. If he was going to catch hell for being five minutes late, you'd think they would be less inclined to waste even more of his time. But you'd think a lot of things that only occurred in a fantasy world. Finally, his messenger went off and Dex was summoned into the office.

It wasn't really a suite, as such. Sure, the managers had offices with walls and doors and they had their own private break room and lav. But the offices themselves were tiny. They had room for a couple of chairs facing each other over a small table. And there was, inexplicably, a coat rack. The managers each had their own tiny rooms, so why would they need space for more than one coat? It was one of those mysteries of life in a firm that Dex expected he would never solve.

Marian signaled for Dex to sit and he followed the order. They sat in silence for a few minutes and Dex studied his boss. He hadn't had much interaction with Marian, really; most of their communication had been one way — top down — and in the form of the firm's internal feed. Dex didn't really know what to expect, so he figured the best tactic was to shut the hell up and wait for his supervisor to make the first move. Eventually, Marian did just that.

"Andersson," his boss began, trying for an air of parental disappointment, "some troubling blips have shown up on my radar lately from your area."

"Oh," Dex said noncommittally, trying to keep things in his boss's court.

"First, there was the cancellation call the other day." Marian's voice was starting to take on that tone that Dex thought of as 'have you tried turning it off and on'- the one you use when you thoroughly believe that the person you're talking to is as bright as a food brick, but you're trying really hard to hide it. "I know you're aware of the policy — no cancellations unless the call is over ten minutes long and no cancellations without a call. That call was three minutes and forty-two seconds long and the recording shows you didn't even try to retain the customer."

Marian paused and Dex knew that he was expected to make

some excuse here. He stayed mum and waited. Marian looked at him and shifted slightly while waiting for an answer, then, finally, after the silence had gone on too long, continued. "Yes, well, that was definitely not acceptable and then the very next morning, six minutes late for your shift." Marian shifted closer to the table between them, leaning in toward Dex. "Six minutes! You know that those are both serious infractions. I don't understand. Up until now your work has always been in compliance with the standards — you've been one of my better employees. Do you have any explanation for this?"

Dex looked his supervisor straight in the eyes and said, "No. No excuses, no explanations. I did cancel the customer's account before the required call time and I was late yesterday. I accept responsibility."

Marian looked even more confused than when Dex was giving the silent treatment. Obviously, most people who got called on the carpet tried to weasel their way out of the consequences. Dex couldn't be bothered; this was all a waste of his time and he just wanted it over with.

"Well," Marian said, trying to gain control back, "the regulations are fairly clear that a combination of errors like these should result in dismissal."

"That's my understanding," Dex said, calmly. Dex thought it looked like Marian had stopped breathing. His boss's face had taken on a slightly purple tint and Dex was wondering if he would have to call one of the in-house medical staff. Obviously his boss was not used to firing people who don't argue.

Marian eventually took a breath. "But, ah, under the circumstances," Dex tried not to smirk, "and given your excellent history with the firm, I think we can deal with the call only and let the six minutes go. You'll be required to make up the time, of course."

"Of course," Dex said, somehow managing to keep the building laugh out of his voice.

"Now, the call." Marian's face took on a stern look. "I can't let you get off scot-free there. The rules are specific here; I'm sorry. My hands are tied. You'll be put on three-quarters time at three-quarters pay for six months." Marian waited for a gasp of shock or an attempt to negotiate, but all Dex could think was that this was ideal. He'd be keeping his apartment and he just wouldn't have to go into B&B as often. He didn't care about the money, so the outcome couldn't have suited him better. He'd just have to figure out how to extend it beyond the six months. Time to bone up on the disciplinary regulations.

"Fine," Dex said, as he stood to leave. "Is that all?"

Marian stood as well, scrambling to understand Dex's reaction. "Yes, Andersson, that's all. Now, today I'll need you to make up the six minutes for yesterday and as of tomorrow you'll have a new schedule. Make sure you check your messages before leaving tonight."

"Will do," Dex said and deciding to throw his boss a bone, added, "thanks," as he walked out of the office.

• • •

Dex spent the remainder of the work day taking calls and chatting with Annabelle about the code that she'd taken off the bot that tried to shoot him. Dex put off contacting her, not knowing what her reaction would be after their terrible date and frankly the thought of talking to her made his stomach knot a little. He eventually had to bit the bullet, though; he wasn't willing to have to slog through the code himself. Dex was no programmer — there was a reason why his day jobs topped out as a CSR.

He pinged Annabelle and feeling his face flush hot when he heard her voice said, "Hi. It's me. Er, it's Dex."

"Well, hello," Annabelle said, her voice taking on the happy tinkle Dex realized he'd come to enjoy when talking to her. "I have to admit, I'm a little surprised to hear from you."

"Yes, well," Dex said, glad that none of his near co-workers was looking his way.

"You haven't changed your mind already," Annabelle said, that tinkle getting even more playful now. Before Dex could stammer out some response, she continued, "Now, that was unfair of me, I know. I just can't help it. Old habits die hard and all that. Now what can I do for you? It's about the multi case, right?"

Dex sighed and admitted that it was, indeed, a business call. He reminded himself how lucky he was to have such an understanding person for an admirer. Once they started talking about the work, he found almost all traces of the awkwardness and embarrassment he'd felt disappear. Unfortunately, Annabelle hadn't really gotten anywhere terribly useful in her analysis of the code. She was now certain that there was no tracing the author of the code based on any information she had at the time. All she did have was the impression that the programmer was pretty sophisticated.

"That bot wasn't executed as elegantly as Ivy's code for the multis," she told Dex, "but the principle is the same and that's not easy to do at all. Hell, there's a reason that Ivy was getting all the avatar work. It's a niche skill, let me tell you."

"So, I should be looking for a competitor of hers, then?" Dex asked.

"If there is one, yeah," Annabelle answered, "and you're definitely looking for someone with a similar skill set. But that's about all I've got for you. Sorry I couldn't help you out more."

"You've been great," Dex said, meaning it. "I don't know where I'd be without you."

"I'd be happier hearing that if you were actually with me," Annabelle said, then quickly said, "I'm sorry. I don't need a harassment charge laid against me. I'll knock it off."

Dex laughed. "Don't worry, kiddo," he said, "I could use a little harassment every now and again. Reminds me of what I'm missing."

"Aw jeez, Dex," Annabelle said, "now you've made me all depressed again."

"Don't be," he said, "I'm fine. You worry about finding yourself a better object of harassment than this pathetic old man, okay?"

"All right," Annabelle said, "you call me if you need me, yeah?

"Sure thing."

• • •

Dex made up his six minutes and ensured he checked his updated schedule for the next day. They had him starting an hour and a half later, which couldn't have been more ideal if he'd made the change himself. He updated his personal system then and there — personal alarm, apartment temperature control and window shades all got moved ahead by ninety minutes. Dex started to wonder if his day could possibly get any better. He headed out of the CSRs room and out of the B&B building.

The rain had stopped in the night and so far it had stayed away. He walked to the train stop and caught the first nearly empty car that came by. As he was en route back to his apartment, the sky began to darken and his stomach began to growl. It might be a two brick night he thought, mentally planning his evening. He wanted to talk to Stella Bish again, feel her out about some of the other people she knew in the underground marketplace. Maybe she had a line on another programmer in Ivy's league. Dex pinged her as he stepped off the train and headed to his building. He was just about to open the main door, when he heard the sounds of shouting around the corner. He pulled up the Cubicle Men's street squad schedule and saw that he was the closest to the scene. Nothing wrong with a bit of off duty action, he thought and began walking toward the sound.

He rounded the corner of his building and heard the shouts again. He picked up the pace and came upon a small streeter cowering behind a dumpster. A pair of larger men were throwing rotting garbage on the whimpering creature and occasionally kicking the prone form. Dex fell back on old lessons learned in the goon squad and made directly for the larger of the two assailants. He kicked the man squarely between the legs, then brought his clasped hands up on the man's nose as he doubled over.

He sidestepped to avoid the man's inevitable fall into a crumpled heap and threw his full weight into a roundhouse punch at the other man. This time the connection was less solid, but seeing his compadre retching in the gutter as blood and snot bubbled from his broken nose seemed to be enough to convince the other guy to take off, which he did. Dex walked over to the stinking, beaten person behind the dumpster, offering his hand. The figure looked up at him and Dex saw that it was an older looking woman. Most people never looked over thirty-five, regardless of their chronological age, so her lined face stood out.

She was sobbing and muttering softly to herself. Dex had to lean in close to hear what she said and the smell of her was enough to wake the dead. "They called me old meat," she said, between her tears, "old meat that belongs in the trash."

"It's okay," Dex said, helping her clean off the garbage from her filthy clothes. "You'll be okay now. Do you have a gang, anyone you stay with out here?" he asked.

"Yes," she said, sniffling, "but we got separated. I think I can find them again." She wiped her eyes with the backs of her grimy sleeves and allowed Dex to help her to her feet.

"I'll have some people come walk with you," Dex said, having already pinged the local goon squad. "They'll be here soon and they'll help you find your people."

"Thank you," she said, a new set of tears forming in her one clear eye.

"No problem, ma'am," he said, as a couple of the local squad arrived in the alley. Dex gave them a brief rundown of the situation and the man lying in the alley began to moan. "They'll take care of you," he said, as the woman began walking out of the alley with her escort. Dex walked back to his apartment building and as he spiraled his way up to his room, wondered if that's what his problem was. That he was just old meat.

# FOURTEEN

THE SHINE HAD worn off the day, somehow. Dex hadn't thought that putting the beat down on a couple of public assholes would destroy his good feeling and it probably wasn't actually that which had done it. It was the assholes themselves and what they had done to that poor woman that made Dex feel like shit. He never would understand what it was about some people that made them think that a good way of dealing with people who were different from them was to assault them.

Back in his apartment, Dex changed out of his now very dirty uniform and poured a drink. His messenger was bleeping away and he saw that it was Stella Bish responding to his question from earlier in the day. Dex went back and forth in his mind, finally shutting off the notification and going offline. He grabbed the bottle from the counter and gave it a long hard look. After a few moments, he shook his head, then drained his drink and refilled the glass. He took the glass and bottle to his chair and pulled up an old video.

The drinking started before they had even finished packing Maksym's stuff in the crate. Dex started watching at the point when he'd opened the bottle. He saw his younger self pour a couple of large glasses and top them off with splashes of real ginger beer. It was an expensive luxury he'd indulged in as a celebration. He saw his hand tremble slightly as it recapped the bottle.

He handed a glass to Maks, who took it with a wide smile. Dex could see three tiny wrinkles around each eye when he smiled. He wondered now if Maks ever had them removed. as he watched them work together packing the crate with Maksym's stuff. "I guess I won't need much of this stuff," Maks said, putting his few clothes into the crate. "They give you a uniform and they're actually not that bad looking." Dex hadn't answered. Maks sat on his bed, looking up at Dex, who was holding a jacket. "It will be fine, Andy," he said, "you'll see. The work is interesting enough and they'll give you your own apartment. No more waiting for the lav, no more labeling your food bricks, no more scrounging for funds."

"I guess," Dex had mumbled, turning away from Maks. Now, in the viewer, he saw the wall of Maksym's room, the wall that had divided their small apartment. His own bed had been on the other side of the thin metal partition. Maks had painted a mural on his side, an abstract of reds and yellows, all circles and triangles. "You should take this," Dex had said, pointing at the divider. "Put it in your new place."

"Yeah," Maks agreed. "It would look nice." Dex saw his own chest heave on the video as he had breathed in deep. He saw himself turn and put the jacket softly in the crate. He focussed on Maks, raised his glass and said, "Let's put on some tunes." Maks smiled and stood. They walked the few paces into the shared area and Maks poked at the interface for the speakers. Music came thundering out and Dex closed his eyes, just has he had at the time. He let the song wash over him; with it came the feelings he'd had then, the feelings he'd never lost.

They were going to be different. Together they had thought they could avoid the mundane life everyone else ended up with. They had made out okay on part time or under the radar jobs. They found someone who would rent them a place for cash money, they had enough for food and cheap booze and they had music. When they had first met on one of the boards where people talked tunes, they'd hit it off immediately. And when they discovered that they actually lived in the same city, it was like fireworks. For a year they lived together, making and playing music, staying up all night talking and listening, as if it were hundreds of years ago when art mattered. They could have lived that way forever. At least, Dex thought they could.

But Maks started to get restless, started talking about getting a real job, with a firm, with benefits. It didn't happen overnight and by the time he actually moved out he had even convinced Dex that it was the right thing to do; that things didn't have to really change just because they'd have more money and separate apartments. But that night, the night he left, Dex knew it was the end. He'd been recording some of their times together — just an hour at a time, but that day got his first disk upgrade and that night he set up his first full time recording.

He stopped the vid and drained his drink. He sat in silence for a few minutes, then got up, used the lav, poured another drink and sat back in the chair.

• • •

Dex sat at his work station at B&B, fingers dancing in front of him as he negotiated the various labyrinths within the B&B system. His own system, though, was going through Stella Bish's message of the previous night. She hadn't been entirely forthcoming — there were no names or links to be found in the message. She had, however, agreed that there were a few people she could recommend for work that was comparable to Reuben's. She was having to scramble to get some of the contracts she'd lined up for Reuben fulfilled elsewhere, but there were a few comparable programmers in her stable, so it was just a matter of time. It wasn't gold, but her information was better than nothing.

Dex decided to do some poking around on his own. He wanted to know just how plugged in to the underground economy Bish was. He started where Ivy had also begun, with Alvaro Zuccarelli. He linked into Marionette City and headed straight for Zuccarelli's offices. No appointment this time. When he walked into the inner office, Zuccarelli looked up as if he were expecting Dex. The guy seemed to be unflappable, but it could just be the avatar's programming.

"I need your advice," Dex said, not waiting for an invitation to sit.

"Of course," Zuccarelli said, gesturing for Dex to continue.

"If I needed some work done," he said, "you know, on the QT, where should I start looking?"

"Well, now, that depends on exactly what kind of work you'd want done, doesn't it."

"Let's start with the kind of work Reuben did."

Zuccarelli looked at Dex suspiciously. "I suppose that suggesting you get Ivy to do it isn't quite the answer you're looking for."

"Correct," Dex said.

"Well," Zuccarelli said, "the main clearinghouse for underground programming is a woman named Stella Bish. I'm surprised you haven't heard of her — I'm fairly certain that Mr. Cobalt had some kind of contract with her."

"You never mentioned that before," Dex said, his eyes narrowing.

"Indeed, not," Zuccarelli replied. "Like I said, I'm not sure. Mr. Cobalt and I didn't discuss his personal business, Mr. Dexter. However, very little off the books work gets done without Ms. Bish in the middle of it."

"Did she negotiate your deal with Ivy?" Dex asked, indicating the building in which they found themselves.

"No," Zuccarelli said. "That was a private arrangement. But, of course, I already knew of Ivy's work. Ms. Bish offers a guarantee to clients that is hard to pass up."

"What do you know about her?" Dex asked.

"I know that she is not one of my clients," Zuccarelli said, haughtily, "so I am much less disinclined to discuss her with you than I might have been otherwise." All of a sudden, Dex had the frightening thought that Zuccarelli was not actually trying to be difficult, that it was just the man's nature to be obstinate. "No one seems to know what her background is. She doesn't seem to have any useful skills — she's not a graphics person or a programmer. However, she appears to have been active in Marionette City from the beginning and she's always been using it to line her pockets." Zuccarelli sniffed disdainfully.

Dex raised an eyebrow and Zuccarelli seemed to instantly pick up his meaning. "Yes, I know," he said, voice heavy with irony, "coming from a glorified loan shark, that seems rich, right?" Dex kept quiet and Zuccarelli continued. "First, I'm not as much a slave to lucre as you might think and second, most of us who've been here for a while remember when there was a lot of community in M City. We used to help each other, discuss things; it was like this was an escape from the world of business, not an extension of it. She was never like that. It was always a business opportunity for her, right from day one.

"In a way, we all owe her a debt. She was the business pioneer here and she paved the way for the rest of us. The trouble is, if you do any high end work, it's a one horse town. Either you contract with Bish, or you're scrounging for the scraps she leaves behind. And she's not proud — it has to be a really bad job for her to turn it down."

"So anyone with any skills will be working for Bish?" Dex asked.

"Yes and no," Zuccarelli answered. "She likes to play both sides against the middle, so there are plenty of people queued up to get into her stable. She only keeps a few names on her radar at a time and it's worth a good amount to be one of them."

Dex thought for a moment. "So, Reuben's death has left a void on her list, then. One that more than a few people might want to fill."

"My god," Zuccarelli said, "you don't think someone killed him for his job, do you?"

"I don't think anything," Dex said, "but can you tell me some other reason someone might want him dead?"

• • •

Dex linked out of Marionette City and was pleased to discover that his B&B workday was done and he still had a good amount of day left. He resolved to commit minor infractions on the job more regularly. He caught the train back to his apartment and once he arrived he spent a good hour on the programmer's boards. The vast majority of the posts went whizzing past Dex's head with a small sonic boom, but clever use of the find function netted a handful of posts about acquiring independent employment. Stella Bish's name was abundant.

It looked like Zuccarelli had been on top of the situation — if you weren't on Team Bish, it was nigh unto impossible get work as an independent. And the wait list to get on with Bish was longer than seemed really reasonable. He could imagine how someone who was desperate might see how the strategic placement of malicious code might help them get ahead. He scraped the boards for any posts relating to independent contracting and started a script to scan them for names, contact numbers, anything that might be useful. In the meantime he linked back into Marionette City and headed for Uri Farone's upgrade parlour.

Dex told himself that he was on the clock and that his only reason for visiting Farone was that he was a connection to Bish. He intended to pose as a potential customer and try and get Farone talking. He wasn't really going to buy anything. Not today, anyway.

Farone's kiosk was in a highly industrial area of Marionette City — it was all virtual clothes and online services for as far as the eye could see. Dex found Software Memory Upgrades sandwiched between a virtual penis enhancement place and an alibi services outfit. As if that didn't tell you everything you needed to know about the world. According to the schedule posted on his board, Farone himself should be staffing the booth. Dex entered the small room and looked around.

The space was small, with just enough room for a couple of clients on the public side of the place and a single staffer on the back end. The wall space was covered with images that a client could touch and get links to audio or video files showing the heartwarming stories of satisfied customers. There was the man who was pained by memories of an error on the job that cost him a promotion. Farone's people excised the memory and now the guy's supposedly happy and successful at work, no longer paralyzed by the fear of making the same mistake. Or the woman who changed the fifty-year old memory of her sister's last days before a fatal accident to include the words "good-bye". All very innocuous and nice and the kind of thing you'd find on a greeting card. Dex wondered just how many upgraded memories were really this innocent.

The avatar behind the counter looked up as Dex moved around the space touching things and consuming the ads. Once Dex had exhausted the promotional material on display, the counterman smiled and opened a private chat channel between them. The name icon on the chat pane indicated that this was, indeed, Uri Farone. "Interested?" he asked.

"Could be," Dex said, wandering over to the counter. "It looks impressive," he said, jerking his head toward the nearest promo link. "How does it work, exactly?"

"Well," Farone said, "if I told you that I'd be giving you the keys to the castle, now wouldn't I?" He smiled disarmingly and

Dex returned the grin without feeling. "But what you need to know is this — we start by altering any media records you have of the event — audio, video, text. Then you come in for personal treatment, which uses a combination of hypnosis, programming and sleep therapy. We can provide references, if you'd like to hear personal experiences of the after effects."

"Sounds intriguing," Dex said, his system receiving the file of contact names that the other man offered. "What's the catch?"

The man across the counter smiled his salesman's grin again. "Well, there are some particular issues with this type of service," he said. "First, there isn't really any way to reverse it. Not because we can't do it, but because you can't, in any true sense, ask us to."

"Why not?" Dex asked.

"When you sign up for the service," Farone said, "we require a very detailed request order for what you want. We need to be clear down to the smallest detail what we are to remove and what we are to add. This is for liability concerns, obviously, but it also is in the client's best interest. It forces you to be sure about what you want and what you expect. Clearly, if you have no memory of what you want us to restore, you can't give us clear instructions to restore it."

"Hmfph," Dex grunted. "That sounds like an overly complex way of saying you just don't want to do it."

"Maybe," the man said, "but you really don't know what you're consenting to. You say, 'I don't like this new memory, make it the way it used to be,' but you no longer even know what it was. We used to allow reversals, but too many people ended up even more unhappy and there are only so many times you can go back and forth with the same customer and the same memory. So, now our contract requires you to trust yourself, to believe that you really want to change your past."

"Okay," Dex said, "I can buy that. What about time frames? Is this a five minute, in and out job, or would I need to book holiday time to get it done?"

"That depends. An erasure takes about a day — we can do a full replacement in a weekend, no problem. If you're just looking for some detail changes, it can range from a half hour to a half day. And there's some prep work as well, so you'd have to budget for a few shorter meetings in advance of the final treatment."

"I see," Dex said. "Well, that brings me to the big question. Cost. If I wanted, say, a removal, what would that run me?"

The proprietor quoted a price and Dex whistled low. "But, of course, you can't put a price on your past, now can you?" Farone said. "Memories are priceless, after all."

"Apparently not," Dex said aloud in his room. To Farone he said, "So you're the man in charge here, right?"

Farone seemed a bit taken aback, but answered, "Yes. It's my shop."

"I thought so," Dex said. "Stella Bish game me your name. And I'm kind of surprised, because I thought she just dealt with contractors." Dex indicated the kiosk with his avatar's gestures. "You seem to be pretty independent here."

"Ah," Farone said, sighing. "You must be the detective."

"Guilty," Dex said.

# FIFTEEN

URI FARONE SUGGESTED that they retire to the "back room." Dex agreed and they linked into a small but impressively decorated office with a few expensive-looking chairs and fully functional liquor cabinet. Dex quickly excused himself and went offline to refill his glass and empty his bladder, then rejoined Farone in his office. Farone was clearly still in sales mode and he couldn't blame the man. Bish had obviously mentioned Dex to him in passing and guys like Farone could smell a mark a mile away. Still, Dex had to give the man credit for being willing to have a conversation. Though at his prices, a single sale would be well worth a chat and a few glasses of virtual single malt.

"These days people think of Stella as just a project manager," Farone said, "but what she does is a lot more complicated than that. Sure, she's the middle layer in a lot of fairly simple transactions — I want a widget, you make widgets, Stella gets us together and takes ten percent. It's a time honoured model and pretty much everyone is happy with it."

"But what about the widget makers she doesn't play with?" Dex asked.

"Well, there is that," Farone said, sipping his scotch. He seemed to savour the moment, then tipped the glass toward Dex. "You sure you don't want effects?"

"I'm sure," Dex said.

"Okay." He paused, Dex guessed that he was running the

conversation back to remind himself of where they left off. "It's surprisingly competitive in here," he continued, "and everyone knows that Stella's people are the best. Not to mention that it's just easier to deal with one known quantity rather than try and dig up someone yourself to do the work for you."

"You seem to be doing all right," Dex said, "and it certainly doesn't look like you need Stella Bish to get work."

"No, I don't," Farone said, "not anymore. But I wasn't always in the memory enhancement biz. I used to be a code monkey just like a million other schmucks out there. But I was lucky. I got on with Stella and was successful enough that I was able to quit my day job. Then I had the time to develop my pet project and eventually quit Stella's gigs, too."

"And that was okay with her?"

"There was a line up of guys banging down the door looking for work behind me," Farone said. "Stella isn't exactly hard up for people. Besides, she gets a kickback every time I get a referral from her, so she's still in the loop."

Dex smiled. "So she's really the lynchpin of the underground economy here, isn't she?" he asked.

"There isn't a whole hell of a lot that goes on without her," Farone agreed, "and a place in her stable is almost a guarantee to get out of the work a day world out there. After a couple of years most people have made enough money and contacts that they are free to live almost exclusively online. There's even a rumour that she's building a giant apartment complex in Europa for the staff."

"Just how many people does she have on the payroll?" Dex asked.

"It's not a payroll," Farone corrected. "They're all independent contractors."

"Right, whatever," Dex said. "How many?"

"Let me see. Give me a second." Farone's avatar stopped animating and stared disconcertingly just past Dex's right ear. In a moment, he flickered back to life and said, "Looks like it's about 143, give or take."

"Oh," Dex said. "You, ah, happen to have a staff list there?"

"Yeah," Farone said, "you want it?"

Dex was in two minds about whether Farone was toying with

him. Not that it mattered if he actually could get a list, so he simply said, "Yes."

"Okay, then," Farone said and pinged Dex's system. He accepted the download and felt the brief weight in his head. "There's a list of people waiting to get on, too. I'll send you a link." Dex wondered how he managed not to find any of this information until now. That was the trouble with instantly accessible information — you still needed to know what you wanted before you could find it.

Dex took a pull on his impotent virtual drink. "So, I have to say that everything you've told me makes me wonder how working for her is any different from working for a firm," he said.

Farone was silent for a moment, then said, "It's the hope, I guess. The hope that one day you get to call your own shots, that you can live the way you want. Maybe it's just a change of pace. But it seems different when you're living it. And a few of us do get out, get to do our own thing."

Maybe, Dex thought. Back in the privacy of his room, he shook his head, clearing the thoughts from his mind. He spent a few more moments talking with Farone and took the custom price sheet the man prepared for him. Linking out of Marionette City he wondered what kind of freedom it was that leaves a person bound to a different master.

• • •

Dex stood and stretched his legs. He finished his drink and refilled the glass with water. He stood and brought up the staff list in his viewer. The price sheet for Farone's memory upgrade was still open and the list partially covered it. Dex scanned the names, stopping at Reuben Cobalt. Out of curiosity, he skipped down to the end. Velarian, Ventner, Vespa... no Velasquez. No news there. As far as Bish was concerned, Ivy was a non-entity.

Dex refocussed on his physical surroundings and stood. Not having any other outlet for the strange feeling in his body, he began pacing. He didn't stalk around his apartment often, but he was getting restless. He could feel very old, very well hidden patterns trying to reassert themselves. Dex grabbed a jacket and fled the apartment. He stepped on the down lift platform and as it lowered him to the ground floor, the desire to pour another rum and fire up the video viewer strongly imposed itself onto his mind. He pushed it aside and stepped into the dark twilight.

• • •

Dex walked down the street, aimlessly moving forward, feet pounding the sidewalk. There were few people on the street, mostly city folks moving from work to home as quickly as possible with hardly any stops in between. Looking closer, Dex saw the usual street dwellers, people like the old woman he encountered the other night, huddling in groups in the corners and potholes of the city. He walked down the street, looking for any public place, somewhere where people might gather together. He knew there were others like him, people who just couldn't get everything in a virtual wrapper, people who needed the funk of real flesh. There were bars where they met, in every town. He knew there were some right there, in his city.

He walked for a half hour, headed for Green Sector. He had tried to forget the goon squad's report a few weeks previously of a gin joint in that neighbourhood that served the real stuff — booze, food and drugs. It was not the kind of place a good guy would usually be found, but its description had reminded Dex of his old hangouts. He nearly missed the door, but he could smell the heady fragrance of smoke, cooking and human armpits. He pushed open the door and the sound of the place froze him in his tracks. People. Live and in the flesh. People talking, arguing, singing, crying. The whole human gamut of it all. And it took Dex's breath away.

He must have been standing in the doorway for some time, because he didn't move until a large man with a dirty beard shouldered his way past him. The big man roughly pushed his way out the door, knocking into Dex as they passed. He scowled at Dex and mumbled something about getting out of the way, but Dex didn't notice any of that. His attention was focussed on the part of his shoulder the man had grazed on his way out the door. The man was long gone, but Dex could still feel his touch as if his flesh had been singed. He couldn't remember the last time someone had touched him. His vision blurred.

It was too much. He turned around and blindly banged out the door and into the night. It had started raining again and Dex turned his face up to the sky to let the cold drops wash over him. He walked back to his apartment in a daze, wondering if there was anywhere in any world that would ever feel like home to him again. The only time he ever felt even close to comfortable was when he was working a case or lost in his memories. He got back to his apartment and dried off in the lav, thinking about his life. Every time he craved companionship, he just opened up the bottle and one of those files. And, why should this day be any different? Once he was dry, Dex poured his drink, sat in the chair and watched.

• • •

The next day, Dex awoke, got himself off to work and pinged Stella Bish. He'd had enough of asking questions behind her back; it was time to get to the source. He asked for a meeting in Marionette City and she eventually agreed, after several attempts to avoid it. She seemed willing enough to talk to him — she'd offered to have a voice or text conversation, but oddly enough Dex wanted the full 3D deal. She finally acquiesced and they'd agreed to meet that evening at the open marketplace.

Dex spent the workday alternately handling irate B&B customers and poking around the boards for independent programmers. He posed as a client looking for some custom work in Marionette City and tried to see whose name floated to the top. The first few boards he came to were more focussed on M City society, so the posters there just pointed Dex to pre-existing businesses operating in Marionette City. He hinted that he was looking for something special, but no one there had any information for him — at least nothing they were willing to share.

From there, he found some links to another board that dealt with the programming behind Marionette City. Here the talk was well beyond Dex's limited knowledge, but he suspected that he might be on the right track. The trouble was that they had a strict non-commercial rule about the posts, so he couldn't just barge in and start soliciting programmers. He decided to take a chance. He sent a message to the moderator of the board explaining that he knew the board was non-commercial, but he was looking to engage the services of someone competent and was hoping that he could get a link to somewhere that would allow him to post his request.

Dex was forced to endure two full customer calls before he got a reply from the moderator. First, the mod had suggested that Dex contact someone who specialized in this sort of thing and had even included a direct link. Unfortunately, it was for Stella Bish. The mod did, however, also include a link to a board that was described as "Mostly full of crap, but you might get some joy there. Good luck, you'll need it."

Dex paged over to the board and had to admit that the mod was right. It was more or less unmoderated and pretty close to chock full of ads for stuff few people would admit to wanting. There were the ubiquitous virtual genital enhancements, with full three dimensional imagery to go with each ad, not to mention the strippers, hookers and "full featured fantasy play vacations." Dex wondered if a link over to this board might help explain to Annabelle why he found virtual intimacy so off-putting.

He spent a long time scouring the boards for anything legitimate, but Dex was getting nowhere in a great hurry. There were only so many graphic images of the various body parts he could buy or rent that he could stand. He spent a few moments cobbling together a script that would strip out the obvious crap and just leave him with the other posts. It would take a few minutes to run, so Dex just set it and forgot it.

He went back to his cranky callers and placated, mollycoddled, argued and cajoled until his new and improved abbreviated workday was done. His script finished running during the train ride back to his neighbourhood and he saved the results to a separate file. He wouldn't have time to work through it all before his meeting with Bish, so he set a reminder for later that evening to bring up the file and see if he could make anything of it.

Dex had a few minutes before he was scheduled to meet with Stella Bish and he used the time to take care of some physical world maintenance that he knew he'd let slide. He set the apartment to clean itself the next day when he was at work and found all the nutrient bar wrappers, bottles and cans that had collected in his apartment over the last weeks. He took them all out to the hall and dumped them into the apartment building's communal recyclatron. Back in his apartment, he changed, poured a drink, went online and made his way to the market. He turned up to the meeting place early and sat on a bench. He watched the virtual birds twittering in a false sky, saw avatars feeding them bits and bytes as they walked hand in hand with their virtual lovers. He almost felt like he was missing out on something, almost felt a little envious. Almost, but not quite.

# SIXTEEN

DEX SAW STELLA Bish coming toward him from what seemed like a mile away. Almost everyone spent so much time on their avatar's appearance, they might as well all be wearing t-shirts that read "Please look at me, aren't I beautiful?" Bish had a slightly different take on that beauty than most of the other folks in the market. Her avatar wore a long, cream coloured dress of a design that aimed to emulate satin. She seemed to be going for an effortless elegance in the midst of leather underpants and bright blue feathered wings.

Fair enough, Dex thought, knowing that his own image with the old fashioned dark suit and hat was somewhat unusual as well. Bish walked through the middle of the plaza, disrupting the birds and turning them into a maelstrom of avian clouds as they squawked and rustled up into the sky. She knew how to make an entrance, Dex had to admit.

She approached the bench where he sat and Dex played along by standing as she approached and touching his hand to the brim of his hat. She might have control over the independent contractors in Marionette City, but she surely didn't have a monopoly on anachronism. She sashayed up to him, a hint of a smile on her lips. "So, gumshoe," she said, "what did you call me up here for?"

Dex gestured for her to sit and she gathered up her skirts, as if to avoid soiling them on some invisible dirt and sat gingerly next to him on the bench. "Seems like you're the go to gal around here," he said, "if you want to get anything personal or interesting made." She smiled and Dex thought he detected a kind of preening expression in the avatar. "No, really," he continued. "It seems like you're the only game in town if someone wants a little extra work." Her smile faded and Dex pressed on. "There isn't a whole lot of independent programming that goes on around here that isn't under your umbrella, is there?"

She held his gaze and her avatar face betrayed nothing. Who knew what was happening autonomically with her physical body. If there was one thing Dex knew, it was that Marionette City was made for liars. "My people are the best," she finally answered. "The market regulates itself. What can I say — people come to a trusted name for a trusted product. There's nothing new here. I offer a kind of guarantee. Who doesn't like that?"

"That's fine," Dex said, "but it seems like there might be people who are so keen to get into your inner circle of contractors that they'd be willing to kill for the job."

She looked taken aback and Dex wondered how many of her expressions were calculated and how many were genuine. "You can't mean that Reuben Cobalt was killed for his contracts? That's..." She paused, as if choosing her next words carefully. "That's both appalling and stupid."

"Only if you don't think about it," Dex said. "You know that Reuben was a multi, right?'

She looked down, then said, quietly, "I had guessed that it was the case." She raised her head and looked Dex straight in the eyes. "I'm not one of those bigots, Mr. Dexter. All I care about in here is my business and I really don't give a damn what people do outside of their working lives. Heaven knows people would be surprised to see my private life. But I don't know anything about Reuben's... uh 'author' doesn't sound quite right. What's the correct term?"

"They usually say 'creator' or 'first'," Dex said.

"Okay," she continued, "his creator. I have no idea who that is. And I couldn't care less. He did fine work, Mr. Dexter. Like you will never know. We lost an artist." She looked away and Dex paused a moment.

"Fine," he said. "Assuming that the killer also knew that Reuben was a multi, maybe it was easier to rationalize. You're not really killing a person, you're just ruining some code. It's not murder, it's vandalism. And if it means the difference between complete obscurity and a solid slate of contract jobs, it might be a reasonable career move."

"Hmm," Bish said, thinking.

"Not so stupid after all," Dex said.

"I'd disagree," she said, "but my perspective is different. At first glance it might appear that programmers are a dime a dozen, but the truly great ones are hard to come by. Sure there are tons of people offering services, but there are only a few who can really make things happen. It takes more than a perfunctory understanding of language — only a few people have the skills to make something new here. I choose my people carefully, Mr. Dexter. That's why my positions are so sought after."

"I understand that," Dex said. "So I have to ask, have you filled the void? Have you replaced Reuben's position?"

Bish looked uncomfortable, but said, "I do have a long list of people waiting for work. Vacancies don't last very long."

"So you have someone in mind for a replacement," he said.

"I do," she answered. "But I do think you're going in the wrong direction."

"That may very well be," Dex conceded, "but I'd still like to see your short list of replacements."

Bish was silent for a moment. "I don't want you harassing my people," she said. "It's bad for business."

"I realize that," Dex said, "but having your staff eliminated can't be good for morale, either."

"Very well," she said, pinging his system for a download. He accepted and a small file transferred over to him. "I trust you will be discreet."

"I'll certainly try," he said, as she rose from the bench. She turned to him and he stood.

"Have you visited Mr. Farone, yet?" she asked.

Dex was taken aback. "I'm sure you know I have," he said.

She turned to walk away and said, over her shoulder, "I hope you find what you're looking for." She linked out of Marionette City without waiting for an response.

Dex opened the file she had sent him and looked at the names. His memory wasn't perfect, but it didn't take long before one name jumped out at him as a familiar one. Sterling Ljundberg, number two on the list. Dex ran through his notes and was reminded that Ljundberg was one of Reuben's buddies from the philosophy boards. And there he was, a contender for Reuben's newly vacated job with Stella Bish. Dex didn't like coincidences much and this one was too great to ignore. Time to talk to Ljundberg again.

• • •

Dex pulled up the contact information he had for Ljundberg, but he got the "not online" message. Fine, it was getting late and not everyone showed themselves online all the time anyway. He paged over to his notes and found a link to the board where he'd first encountered Ljundberg. He ran a search for the man's name and saw that Ljundberg hadn't posted there in some time. In fact, he hadn't posted there since before Dex had spoken to him days earlier. That wasn't entirely unusual; looking at the man's posting pattern, he'd been a sporadic participant for the last few months.

Dex was pretty sure he ought to be able to find out more about Ljundberg, but he didn't have the skills to even figure out where to start. He felt like he was abusing whatever bizarre relationship they had, but he pinged Annabelle anyway, explaining that he wanted any information on Sterling Ljundberg's activities online in the last week. He provided all the contact information he had and sent the message. He figured she'd get it in the morning and get back to him later on, but she answered back right away via voice chat.

"Hey, Dex," she said. "If I didn't know better I'd think you were just making excuses to talk to me."

"I don't need an excuse," Dex lied, "but I do need help. I'm starting to think you should have taken this case off my hands a long time ago."

"Bullshit," she said, "you love this stuff. Besides, I'm no investigator; I'm just a code monkey. This is just one of those times when it takes two to tango, you know?"

"Sure," he said. "I really do appreciate your help, though. I want you to know that."

"I do," she said, softly. "Look, here's the thing. I've written up a search script to see if I can track Ljundberg through my secret back door to the everywherenet. But it's going to take a while to run." She paused a moment. "If you have some free time, you wanna just talk for a bit? No strings, we're just pals — you know, a conversation. If you have the time, of course."

Dex really didn't have anything else to do and with his new work schedule he had more than enough time to hang out with Annabelle if he wanted. What the hell, he thought. He figured he owed her something for all the crap he'd been getting her to do for him, not to mention for being such an asshole the other night. He could probably suck it up and make small talk for a few minutes. "Sure, kiddo." he said. "I'd love to."

• • •

Dex surprised himself. They talked for a good three hours and it wasn't really that bad. Annabelle told him about some of the sneaky ways she tapped into the security sectors of the everywherenet to get information she wasn't really supposed to have. A lot of what she said went over his head, but she was so into it that some of her excitement rubbed off on him and he found himself asking her to explain things he'd never even remotely cared about before. She asked him about investigating and what that was like and he talked about that feeling you get being all wrapped up in a puzzle and having to just poke it at its edges until a little piece comes free, then following it until you get out and can see it for what it is.

Partway through the first hour, Dex refilled his glass and he heard Annabelle do the same. They talked for a while about their day jobs, which was an easy source of bonding. Annabelle was a low level grunt programmer for a major train firm in Europa and she had all the same bullshit in her job that Dex had in his.

"Europa," Dex said, confused. "But you're on my local squad."

"Yeah," she said. "I used to live there, but my firm got acquired by a big Euro outfit and I was transferred. I moved physically, but since I'm not Street I never bothered to switch squads. It's worked out fine, since I'm still more or less on a Namerican time schedule. Everything's virtual anyway, so I've hardly even noticed the change."

They continued to talk shop, comparing strategies for getting annoying people to stop bothering them and coming up with clever ways to tell managers that their ideas were stupid without losing their jobs. Dex shared his recent discovery that if you fucked up just enough, they'd reduce your hours without cutting your benefits and suggested that Annabelle should try it.

"Somehow I doubt I could get away with that," she said, her speech having gotten a little looser as they got further into the night. "You know there's something about you that just makes people want to help you, right?"

"Um," Dex said, laughing, "I actually think it only works on you."

Annabelle snorted and that made Dex laugh even harder. "You totally don't see it, do you?"

"I don't know what you're talking about," he said, trying to get the laughter under control.

"You have this, I don't know, vulnerability combined with menace," she said. "It's a very potent combination. I think it's what makes you such a great investigator. People feel compelled to help you, no matter whether they're motivated by fear or compassion. It's weird."

"No," Dex said, "you're weird."

"Well, I knew that," Annabelle said. "That's why I like you. Dangerous, needy guys turn me on. I never know if they're going to hang me from a meathook and ravish me or curl up in my lap and let me stroke their hair. It's the not knowing what's coming next that's so hot."

Dex didn't know what to say to that and an awkward pause hung between them for a while. He polished off his drink and finally said, earnestly, "I'm sorry I'm not the man you think I am."

Annabelle laughed lightly. "Don't be sorry, you're perfectly wonderful. I just need to remember that I can't make everything I want happen just by wishing it were so. I guess it's an occupational hazard."

Dex laughed again, wondering how she could be so easy with this. He knew how much it hurt to have something you want so badly to be close enough to taste, but only to watch it walk away from you. Quietly, he said, "I wish I could be what you want," but Annabelle wasn't listening anymore.

Instead, she interrupted, excitedly saying, "The script is done! And you're not going to believe this. Unless I somehow fucked this up beyond all recognition, our guy has completely vanished."

# SEVENTEEN

WHAT DO YOU mean, 'vanished'?" Dex asked, incredulous. "People don't just disappear. Hell, even Reuben didn't disappear when he got killed. How can someone disappear?" His voice had risen about an octave from the beginning of the sentence to the end. With a great effort he tried to get himself together. "That's the thing about everywherenet — you're on all the time. It's.... fucking... everywhere. That's the point."

"Dex, calm down," Annabelle said. "People disappear off the 'nets all the time. They die, or they go offline. It's not that unusual."

"Then how come I've never heard of it before?"

"Well," Annabelle said, "ever had a missing persons case?"

"No."

"And have you ever looked for a dead person online."

"Uh, no."

"There you go then," she said, matter of factly. "It's perfectly normal, it just doesn't come up that often."

"Okay, fine." Dex said, "So, you're saying that Ljundberg is dead."

"Or offline."

"What do you mean, offline?"

"You know, offline," she said, starting to sound a bit frustrated. "Not online. Unconnected to the 'nets. Not controlled by or directly connected to a computer or external network."

"I know what the word means," Dex said, with a slight petulant whine. "I just don't see how a person would do that. How would you do anything? You can't go anywhere, buy anything — could you even get into your apartment?'

"Yeah, you could do that," Annabelle said. "Actually you'd be surprised at how much you can actually do offline. A lot more stuff is controlled by that chip in your hand than you'd think. The 'nets are really only for communication and banking and most rudimentary financial transactions, like paying train fare, are actually covered by the chip."

"Huh," Dex grunted. "So, Ljundberg could be offline and busy doing stuff out there in the physical world?"

"Could be," she agreed, "and probably is."

"Can you tell if he's alive or not?"

"It's not conclusive," she said, "but when people are online when they die, there's this really interesting data pattern they sort of expel into the network at the moment of death. It's pretty cool and no one seems to know what it is. But there's none of that recorded for Ljundberg."

"So if he is dead," Dex said, "he was already offline when it happened." Dex thought for a moment. "Any way we can track him, now?"

"I was waiting for you to ask that," she said, glee evident in her voice. "Deep in the everywherenet is the control program that monitors everyone's ID chips. That's what lets us use the same chip to get into work, home, the train, whatever. Now, it's covered in a lot of layers of security, but I've been looking for an excuse to drill into that system for a while now. If I can get in there, I think I'll be able to see where Ljundberg is. Or at least where he's recently been, assuming he hasn't chopped off his hand or gone off to the middle of the ocean on a rickety old raft or something."

"Good," Dex said. "Now, don't let me keep you from this exciting break and enter job of yours." He could almost hear her grin.

"I'll keep you posted," she said and ended the call.

• • •

Dex refocussed on the physical world, stood and stretched and shook his head. He visited the lav and checked the time. Even with the extra ninety minutes of sleep in the morning, it was getting late. He thought he ought to take a slug of SleepingJuice and call it a night. He was wired, though and even though the soporific tonic would knock him out no matter what, he just didn't feel like sleeping yet.

He pulled up the recording he'd made of his conversation with Annabelle. He ran it back to the beginning, before the talk took its turn toward the intimate and disturbing. He listened as they talked about their work, sharing war tales and banter. Dex was surprised to hear his voice have that easy sound, like the conversation was comfortable, like it had been back with Maks.

But then he closed his eyes, listening to her voice tell some funny story about a doomed project at her day job and he tried to picture her. All he could see was her inhuman avatar, sickeningly morphing into different images in an attempt to please him. He opened his eyes and forced himself to picture something else. How could he explain how much that was the opposite of attractive to him, how he didn't care what she looked like, so long as she was real?

He stopped the audio and poured another, though slightly smaller, glass of rum and ginger. He opened up his private files and searched for just the right video. The one from when he first started recoding. When he and Maks were out riding the trains with nowhere to go, high on youth and some drug Dex couldn't even name now. Maks was making an ass of himself, making faces and trying to be funny, trying to get Dex to laugh and "ruin the shot."

There it was — a couple of hours in — the part Dex wanted to see, to remember. On a train going through an outlying part of town, no one else aboard, the two of them wrestling over the last bite of a food brick. Laughing and grabbing at each other, falling over each other from the movement of the train and drug induced lack of coordination, their faces glowing with sweat and pure animal pleasure at movement of muscle. Dex felt his throat tighten and he closed his eyes. He wondered which would be worse, never knowing happiness, or this. The remembering. And he wondered if he ever would have the courage to erase the memories, to start a new life, a life without the burden of the past.

• • •

The next morning, Dex found a message from Annabelle waiting for him when he was on the train. Judging from the time stamp, she'd been up almost all night cracking in to the ID chip tracker.

The good news was that Ljundberg wasn't dead, unless someone had hacked off his hand and was carrying it all over Guadalajara. The bad news was that he was still offline and there was no way to contact him, except physically tracking him down and going to talk to him embodied.

When Dex got to his station at B&B, he pinged Annabelle. He figured she'd be dodging morons at her day job, but he got back an automated reply. She'd set her system to send him a specific message if he called, which told him that she was on weekend and was sleeping in. She asked him to message her and said that she'd call him once she woke up. He sent the message and got to work dealing with B&B customers. While he was talking people into extended warranties they didn't need and helping others find the power switch on their new toys, Dex pulled up the intercities train schedules.

The timing was reasonably good, since he'd be on weekend himself the next day. Usually Dex's weekends were either lost in a bottle and a stack of videos on loop or he threw himself bodily into whatever case he was on. This weekend would be an extreme example of the latter. It was a long train trip to Guadalajara, but there was an overnight shuttle and he booked himself on the one leaving that night. He'd have up to three days to find Ljundberg and he didn't know if it was enough time but there wasn't really any other option.

He pinged Ivy. "Is it okay if we just text?" she asked. "I'm out with Renna at a club and I might need to talk there."

"If this isn't a good time to talk, you could just call me back." Dex asked.

"No, it's okay," Ivy answered. "Renna's dancing right now, so we've got a few minutes at least. Any news?"

"Maybe," he answered. "I have to do some physical traveling to follow up a lead. I needed to let you know that there will be some additional expenses associated with the trip."

"That's fine," she said. "Do you need me to add funds to the escrow account?" Dex quickly brought up the figures and saw that the account was still quite healthy.

"That won't be necessary," he answered. "I just needed your authorization to accrue the expenses."

"Consider this a blanket authorization," she said, "to do whatever needs to be done. I'm not concerned about the cost, only about the result."

"Very well," Dex said. "I'll contact you if I learn anything useful."

"Thank you," she said and signed out.

Dex booked his train fare and made a quick list of things he'd need to pack. He pinged Annabelle again, but just got the response she'd set for him again. He hoped he'd get to talk to her before he left. Dex had never gone looking for a missing person before and he wasn't sure if he'd need some kind of special tools or something. He felt very much out of his element, but it was a surprisingly good feeling. This case had been strongly lacking in leads up until now and Dex could almost feel the answer coming to meet him.

This was it, the moment he had talked to Annabelle about. He had poked here and there, asking inane questions of people with no information long enough to finally get a tiny thread. A thread he could grab on to and pull until the whole fabric of this puzzle came apart in his hands. This was his favourite moment, the one that made all the rest of it worthwhile. It even made talking to moronic B&B customers seem less horrible than usual.

The rest of his workday passed by quickly, Dex spending the majority of his thought power on collecting information about Guadalajara — maps, names and contacts for inns and lodges, a schedule for the local transportation. By the time he clocked out of B&B, he was armed with enough travel information to spend a two week holiday there. He caught the train back to his apartment, knowing he had only about an hour to pack before he needed to catch the local train to the intercity station.

Just as Dex was getting off the train and starting to walk to his building, his system pinged. It was Annabelle, finally. "I'm so glad you called," Dex said, "I've got a reservation on the train to Guadalajara in a couple of hours."

"Whoa," Annabelle said, "that was fast."

"No time like the present," Dex said, walking up the front stairs to his building. "Besides, I'm on weekend now, so it's easy to take the time."

"Makes sense," she said, then explained that she had been monitoring Ljundberg and he seemed to be more or less stationary. "I've had very little activity for the past couple of days," she said, "just a train trip here..." she sent a link to a map of the train routes with a stop and line highlighted, "and a purchase here." Another map downloaded to Dex's system, this time showing a small store just off the line about half a klick to the north. "He must be staying somewhere near there, but I don't have anything more specific for you, I'm afraid."

"No, that's fantastic," Dex said, now in his apartment, cramming a couple of changes of clothes into a small shoulder bag. "Can you keep me posted of any changes?"

"Of course," Annabelle said. "I wouldn't have it any other way. But you keep in touch, yourself, okay?"

"Will do," Dex said and ended the call. He set his apartment for no occupancy for the next three days and as he walked past the box, grabbed a handful of food bricks to stick in his bag. He left the apartment, rode the lift down to the street and headed out to the train.

# EIGHTEEN

DEX INTENDED TO spend the time on the train studying his maps, researching Ljundberg and maybe catching a quick nap. He managed a little of each on the four hour trip, with the exception of the nap, but ended up staring out the window most of the time. The train moved quickly on its magnetic levitation rails, but Dex seemed to be endlessly fascinated by the landscape whizzing past. Of course, the train made a few stops along the way and Dex gawped openly at the unfamiliar cities and people.

When the train slipped into its berth at the station, Dex gathered his things and ensured that everything was safely tucked into his bag, then he slung it over his shoulder so that it clung tightly to his chest. He walked out of the station and pulled up the overview map Annabelle had sent him. There was a local train stop a block north of the intercity train station and he set to walking toward it. If he took the local up a while, he could get off at the station closest to the kiosk where Ljundberg's chip had last registered.

Even though it was nearing midnight, the crowds were thick at the local train stop. It looked like a two train wait to Dex when he arrived, joining the mass of people that were more like a throng than a queue. When the train arrived and its doors melted away, he moved forward with the teeming mass. More people crammed themselves into the car than he ever would have dreamed possible, but he wasn't among them. The doors re-materialized, blocking out the unlucky and locking in the, perhaps, even more unlucky. The train sped away and Dex looked around him wondering how people lived like this every day.

He had always lived in a smaller centre and this was the longest trip he'd ever taken. He and Maks once traveled to the next city over for a weekend party and Dex had been as taken with train travel then as now. There was something about seeing all those other places, full of other people, whipping past at over five hundred K — it was one of the few times Dex ever felt hopeful about the world. It seemed like all those people, so close yet so distant from each other, just going about their daily lives, held the most amazing potential in the universe. The utter normalcy of it all amazed him.

Here in Guadalajara, though, that same crush of humanity, in their banal daily existence, almost suffocated him. Dex worried that he wouldn't be able to handle even the short train ride, but when the next train arrived, he was swept up in the blind human momentum and into the car. He was aboard and the doors closed before he even had a chance to think about escaping. Once the train started moving again, he pulled up his map and set his system to notify him when his stop was approaching. He rocked back and forth as the light magrail wound its way through the city, held upright by the crush of people on either side of him.

His system pinged him, warning that his stop was approaching and Dex slithered through the crowd toward the door. He barely squeezed out the open side of the car before the door reformed and the train zoomed away. Dex looked around him, at the street and the community he'd traveled so far to visit. There was an eerie sense of familiarity here, the street looking only a little different from a hundred streets Dex had walked before. Tall, anonymous buildings lined the road, which was narrow and clogged with people walking to or from work, the expressions on their faces vacant as they spent most of their attention on some online distraction.

This particular neighbourhood reminded Dex of the area he'd lived in when he lived with Maks, full of old and poorly maintained independent apartment buildings and discount food and booze stores. Dex suspected there would be a couple of bars or game halls nearby, since these run-down communities tended to be home to the physical world entertainment areas. Dex walked north, carefully watching the other people on the street.

On the high speed train south, he'd managed to spend a few productive minutes checking out Mr. Sterling Ljundberg. He got an image capture of the man's avatar from Marionette City, a tall, thin, dark haired man, with shoulder-length hair flowing out behind him. He wore small spectacles, an unusual affectation and had a van dyke beard. Of course, there was absolutely no reason why Ljundberg would necessarily look the same in the physical world, but it was all he had to go on. He'd asked Annabelle to see if she could come up with something more useful, but he hadn't heard from her yet.

Dex pulled up his list of potential accommodations and had his system cross reference it with the local area map. Almost immediately, a spot on the map started to glow with a dull red tint. A faint dotted line appeared, drawing a walking path from his current location to the nearest place he could rent a bed. It was a cheap travelers' inn, but so long as it was clean, Dex didn't care. He was actually pleased that it was a lower class establishment — cost wasn't a factor, since his expenses were one hundred percent billable, but low rent rooms were more likely to have talkative people.

He opened the door to the inn and his system immediately popped up a greeting message. "Welcome to El Presidente Metropol Hotel," the bright banner read. Underneath, room rates and availability were listed and Dex chose a single room with attached lav. His system pinged, notifying him of the first night's rate being withdrawn from his account. The hotel's system gave him a password to enter at the chip writer and Dex dutifully stick his left hand in the machine, then sent the password to its server. After getting his room key programmed into his chip, he followed the map up the lift to his room.

The room was about half the size of his own apartment, holding just a bed and a chair, with a 20 cm ledge along the wall acting as a table. The lav was tiny, but functional and clean and overall Dex was perfectly happy with the space. He stripped, used the lav and set his system to wake him in seven hours. He took a corresponding hit of SleepingJuice and climbed into the narrow bed.

• • •

Dex awoke before his alarm went off, the light from the small window illuminating the room as if he'd turned on the high output LEDs. He sat up, rubbed his face and turned off his system alarm. He padded over to his bag, rummaged around inside it and pulled out a small bottle of Flying Fish. He took a sip, just enough to get the juices flowing and walked over to the window. It was warm in the room and he hadn't found any way to get at the room's system to change the temperature — he wondered if maybe the room wasn't even climate controlled. Dex looked out the window at the dark haze in the sky, turned a light pink by the high sun.

He absent-mindedly rubbed a hand over his flat belly, the muscles beneath firm and defined. The food bricks regulated metabolism and the Flying Fish counterbalanced the booze. Pretty much everyone, except the most physically fashionable, looked like this — lean, muscled and young. Dex had seen a few people around following the most recent trend of having softer bodies, created by complex diets or specialized metabolism supplements, but Dex couldn't be bothered by trends. He didn't even take the Flying Fish for his looks — it was more to just get out of bed in the morning.

There wasn't a lot to see out the window — just the street he had walked up the night before and the facades of the other nearby buildings. It was the colour of the sky that really got to him. Dex wasn't sure he'd ever seen a sky that wasn't grey before. He just stood there, looking at the colour deepen, then fade away and after he'd been at the window about a half hour Dex finally turned and walked into the lav.

He showered, dried off and dressed, then packed up his bag and headed out of the room. He took everything with him, unsure if he'd be returning and took the stairs the three flights down to the lobby area. There was a small kiosk set up with breakfast flavoured food bricks and water and Dex bellied up to its bar along with a handful of fellow guests. A half dozen chairs were set up in the lobby and Dex took a couple of the bars along with a large water bottle over to one of them. Sitting, he tore open the wrapper of one of the food bars and hungrily tore at the sticky mixture contained inside. Washing it down with a swig of water, he turned to look at the other people in the lobby.

As he'd suspected, most of them seemed to be focussed on their physical surrounding, Dex only saw one person with the thousand metre stare that being online generates. He decided to take a risk and turned slightly toward the man sitting in the chair next to him. "Hi, there," he said and saw the other man nod in response. "I just got here last night. Is there anywhere to go hang out here, I mean physically near here?"

His neighbour merely shrugged, mumbling, "Dunno," but a hyper-fashionable, slightly pudgy woman leaning up against the wall across from them said, "There's a place just down the road. The Free Robots Cafe. It's pretty big, they serve palatable coffee and real drinks, but it's usually full of Offline Cleanse types, so if you're not into that sort of thing, it can be kind of annoying."

"Offline Cleanse?" Dex said.

"You know," she said, rolling her eyes, "that new anti-tech fad? It's all over the boards these days." She ate the last bite of her food brick and pitched the wrapper in the recyclatron before heading out the front door. Dex sat back in the chair and went online, searching for information about whatever it was that the woman had mentioned.

The woman had been right, the regular gossip boards were full of posts about the Offline Cleanse. It turned out that a fairly popular vid actor had become fond of the concept and his fans and detractors had gone crazy posting about it. Pretty soon it had hit the radar of the mainstream posters and it seemed to be the topic du jour for most of the big boards.

From what Dex could gather, it was based on your standard luddite ideas — that things were better in the past and that people had lost touch with each other and their own "inner selves" because of the 'nets. The ideas weren't even all that radical — there was no call for people to permanently abstain from the 'nets or remove their implants. The main concept was for what they called "purification days." One weekend a month, adherents were expected to go offline completely. That meant no messaging, no boards, no system generated wake up alarms. It was extreme, but only in the most basic sense and Dex thought three days a month was a pretty low commitment if you really believed that being online was "unnatural" and "dehumanizing".

However, it certainly sounded like a good explanation for

Ljundberg's disappearance. He'd been "missing" for a couple of days now and the Offline Cleanse required complete severance from the online world. Dex paged over to his messages, looking for something from Annabelle. If he could just get a good idea of what Ljundberg looked like, he might actually be able to find him. It seemed like it was time to put in a good long shift at that café.

# NINETEEN

DEX HADN'T HEARD from Annabelle and he was willing to believe that if she found something she'd let him know, so he just paged away from his messages. He refocussed on his physical surroundings and discovered that he was alone in the lobby. He checked the time and was relatively unsurprised to discover that a couple of hours had gone by. The Cleanse propaganda certainly had a point — you could easily waste a lot of time on the 'nets.

He took a drink from the half full water bottle and stuck it, along with his second, uneaten food brick, into his bag. He pushed open the front door and was assaulted by a heat and humidity he'd never encountered outside of a lav. It wasn't actively raining, but Dex could feel drops of water condensing on his skin and he wished he was wearing some lighter, more breathable clothes. He walked up the street looking for Free Robots. He didn't know exactly what he was looking for, but he hoped for a sign or something obvious. He walked up three blocks, getting hotter and wetter with every step and didn't see anything that looked like a café of any kind.

Dex crossed the street and headed back toward El Presidente, still looking for the café. As he was almost directly across the street from his hotel, he realized that while he might be looking for a Cleanser hangout, that didn't mean that he had to take a techno-logical vacation. He paged over to his search program and ran a query for the café. In less than a second his map was glowing slightly from just behind him and to his right. He turned and followed the directions. He stopped as soon as he had caught up to the slight glow and focussed fully on his surroundings. He was next to a fairly short, somewhat derelict looking building. It seemed to be unmarked and its main door opened into what appeared to be the lobby of a private housing complex.

Dex tentatively climbed the outside stairs and pulled on the doorknob. It opened and he found himself in a large vestibule. The locked door to the main lobby was ahead of him, but there were four other doors on either side of him, leading off to what he presumed were businesses. None were clearly marked, but he could hear the sounds of music and people talking from behind the one on his right, closest to the outside door. As he walked toward it, Dex did see a very faint image of the words *Robustezas Libres* imprinted on the metal of the door. He pulled it open and a blast of cool air greeted him. He stepped inside and closed the door against the heat.

It was dark and cool and at first that was all Dex could comprehend. His eyes adjusted to the low light and the mixture of condensation and sweat cooled on his brow and he started to look around. There were several low tables with chairs scattered about the place and the walls were lined with banquettes. The inside wall was taken up with a large bar, behind which were several bottles of liquor and a couple of urns of what Dex assumed by the smell of the place was coffee. He headed for the bar and was surprised to see a handful of food options as well, all of which seemed to be made from real, grown in the ground food.

He wasn't about to experiment with the solids, but he guessed he'd be willing to try the stuff in the urn. He ordered a coffee from the touchpad at the bar and a stiff metal arm shot down from the ceiling, hooking a cup with a thin extremity and drawing the dark brown liquid into it. The arm then swung the cup carefully around to where Dex was standing and placed it on the bar. The whole process took about ten seconds.

Dex took his cup and made his way to an empty table in a corner where he could see the room. It was about midday and he guessed that the place was half full. The tables were mostly occupied by one or two people, most of whom were silent and staring.

But a couple of the booths were full with what seemed to be one larger group of people, who were talking animatedly with each other. Dex figured they had to be the Offline Cleanse people the woman earlier had spoken about.

Dex sipped at his coffee, which was strong and bitter and made his heart feel a little funny, but he thought he rather liked it. There were about a dozen people at the two booths across the way and none of them were tall, thin men with long dark flowing hair and a van dyke beard. Dex realized that he couldn't even use gender as guideline, everything being malleable as it is, both online and off. He pulled up his physical control and figured out how to magnify his sight and was truly thankful that he'd stayed off the booze the previous night. The shift in perception was immediate and off-putting and Dex wasn't entirely sure that he wasn't going to throw up even though he was completely hangover-free.

He kept his vision magnified as long as he could, just trying to get a good recording of all the people at the table. After about a minute he had to turn it off and even then he had to keep his eyes closed for a few moments to let the nausea wear itself off. The acidic brew in his cup didn't really help, but it was there, so he sipped at it anyway. Once his stomach had calmed down some, Dex opened his eyes and pulled up his viewer. He isolated the best still images of each person in the group, pulled them out and sent them to Annabelle with a message explaining what he'd found so far — the Offline Cleanse, the café, the people there.

Dex sat at the table, thinking. In his time as a investigator, he'd never been in a situation where he didn't have an idea of the players involved. At a very minimum he had some name, even if it were a false one and he could look up a person's history based on that. This was more like working the goon squad, where everyone was anonymous and you had to just run on instinct. As much as Dex wanted to barge over to the table, shout "Sterling Ljundberg" and see who flinched, his gut told him to wait. His gut also told him to eat something, so he pulled out the second food brick he'd taken from the hotel's kiosk and unwrapped it.

He spent the next half hour eating his lunch, drinking his coffee and watching the Cleansers interact. He wondered if maybe they weren't so crazy. What was so bad about just turning it all off for a couple of days a month and actually talking to people? The thought of it scared him a little, but the more he watched them — smiling, laughing, even touching — the more he liked the idea. It would be impossible for him though, really. Weekends were a gold mine for doing Cubicle Men work and he couldn't afford to be cut off from his clients, the squad, and everything else for three whole days.

He finished his coffee and brought the empty cup up to the bar. The metal arm dropped down, picking up the cup and depositing it into the industrial autoclave. Dex steeled himself for the inevitable temperature change and pushed open the door to the cafe. He headed out the door of the building and walked back to El Presidente. He needed to talk to Annabelle and he figured that he'd probably be stuck here at least another night, so he ought to see about getting his room for another night.

When he walked into the lobby, the "Welcome to El Presidente Metropol Hotel" banner popped up and Dex was able to get the same room again. He took the stairs up, his heart pounding and mind racing. He walked into his room and stripped, then stood under a trickle of water in the lav that didn't last anywhere near long enough before the blower kicked in. He figured out how to manually dim and open the window and stretched out naked on the bed.

Dex didn't think he could possibly have slept, even with SleepingJuice. That coffee was nothing like the swill they served at B&B, which was no surprise, but it was like nothing he'd ever even had before. He thought he could feel every cell in his body twitching, ever so slightly. It wasn't entirely unpleasant, but it made concentrating on anything else somewhat difficult. He forced himself to be productive and pinged Annabelle. She was up and available. He linked into Marionette City and sent her a link to Monte's.

He sat at his usual table, unable to forget his physical body like he usually did when he was in Marionette City. He could feel the slight breeze from the window over his skin and his right leg seemed to have developed a tiny twitch. His avatar was mindlessly sipping an effects-free drink — Dex was afraid what might happen if he started adding more chemicals to the mix. He waited a few minutes, visually and aurally focussed on the lights and music at Monte's while physically focussed on his own body. It was an eerie experience.

Finally, Annabelle walked in. She was dressed more the way Dex was accustomed to seeing her, in a patterned t-shirt and dark pants and she walked over to him grinning. "Hey, Dex," she said, sitting across from him. "It's great to see you again."

"You too," he answered honestly, a shiver trilling its way up his spine. He blinked and composed himself, then asked her if she'd gotten his message from earlier in the day.

"Of course," she answered. "I've just spent the last bunch of time looking up this Offline Cleanse. I'm sad to report that they're a pretty boring group. All they have is a bunch of propaganda boards that say nothing new or enlightening. It's just a couple of high profile people who are into it that caught everyone's fancy. That and the three days off idea. But they don't seem even remotely dangerous."

"I wasn't too concerned about them being dangerous," Dex said, "though you can't be too careful. I didn't think that they were the reason Reuben was killed. I still like a practical, financial motivation better than any ideological one."

"Agreed," Annabelle said, "and Ljundberg definitely has one of those." She grinned and Dex knew she'd found something.

"Well," he said, leaning closer to her, a smile forming on his avatar's lips, "give up the goods. I know you've got something for me. Did you manage to identify Ljundberg out of those images? Do you know what he looks like?"

"Slow down, tiger," Annabelle said, laughing. "No and yes."

"What?"

"I didn't identify Ljundberg in those images you sent," she said, "but I do have an image for you." She pinged Dex's system and an image download came across for him. "Ljundberg wasn't there this morning. I'm sure of it."

"So, why are you grinning like an idiot, then?" Dex asked.

"Because I identified someone else in those images of yours," she said, sending another image to his system. "The short blonde woman in the corner." Dex pulled up the second file she'd sent and recognized one of the more active participants in the group.

"What about her?" he asked.

"I'd guess that she's probably going to be Ljundberg's boss pretty soon, if she isn't already," Annabelle said, leaning back in her chair with a smug smile on her face. "That's Stella Bish."

# TWENTY

DEX DIDN'T KNOW what to say. He was so flummoxed that he even forgot about the caffeine coursing through his body and sat stock still for the first time in hours. "How can that be Bish?" he finally got out. "Keeping time with an anti-tech group?"

"It's her, all right," Annabelle said, the grin still plastered on her face. "I pulled off the highly improbably task of breaking into the central records in everywherenet."

"Central records?" Dex asked. "That's the database that matches biometrics to accounts to ID chips. It's the big box that keeps us all tagged and identified and watched. And I got in." Her voice was almost breathless and although Dex didn't really understand what she was talking about, he could tell it meant a lot to her.

"Good job," he said, smiling. "If anyone could do it, it's you."

"Thanks," she said, her face flushing slightly. "Anyhow, I now have access to the matched set of online identities to physical world images. The first file I sent you is Sterling Ljundberg's most recent facial image. You should have no trouble identifying him. And I ran all the images you sent through a facial recognition program and she came up as Stella Bish."

"It can't be..."

"That's what I thought, too," Annabelle said, interrupting him. "So I looked for her online. Not there. I poked through the history and she disappeared last night. I double checked the biometrics of this Stella Bish against she who rules Marionette City and it was a perfect match. It's her, Dex, there's no doubting it."

"Shit," he said and started thinking aloud. "So if Ljundberg is doing this Offline Cleanse thing, which I guess we don't even know for sure at this stage, he's probably got a connection with Bish other than just business. I mean, they're both here in the same city and it looks likely that they spend time at the same java joint. Which makes me wonder why he isn't already on staff..."

"Good question," Annabelle said, her avatar's face wrinkling into a frown. "And if he'd already pals with the boss, why would he need to get rid of Reuben in order to be next in line?"

"Damn it," Dex said, "'this fucking case. Every time I think I'm getting somewhere, the whole thing turns thirty degrees and I'm tossed around and confused. It's bloody annoying."

Annabelle smiled. "But it's what you love."

"Since when do you know everything about me," Dex asked, scowling. Annabelle looked a little taken aback, then Dex broke out in a grin. "Fine, I love it, okay. Happy now? So let's get to solving this bloody great puzzle, shall we?"

"Okay," Annabelle said, smiling again. "So, what's the plan?"

• • •

When Dex had finished talking to Annabelle, he refocussed on his hotel room to discover that the coffee buzz had worn off and he had gotten unpleasantly cold. He sat up on the bed, stretching his sore muscles. He stood, running his tongue over his gummy and sour mouth. He picked up the clothes he'd earlier thrown on the floor and put them back on. He rummaged through his bag to find the bottle of water from the morning and he downed what was left of it in one go. He vigorously rubbed his hands over his face in an attempt to imbue some energy into his body.

He headed out the door of hotel room and checked the time. It was early evening, which seemed like the kind of time he figured the Cleansers to gather. Of course, it was all just guesswork, but with no way to contact Ljundberg or Bish, Dex had to rely on his gut. He took the stairs down to the ground floor and saw that the brightness of the afternoon sunlight had dimmed somewhat. The ambient light from outdoors was now more like what he was used to. He hoped that the temperature had moderated some as well.

When he pushed open the hotel's main door, the climate wasn't as stifling as it had been that morning — the humidity was lower, though it was still warmer than Dex would have liked. At that moment, though, the heat was taking the chill off of his body that had accumulated while he was in Marionette City with Annabelle and Dex resolved to enjoy the heat for a long as possible.

Dex turned right once he got to the street, heading for the small store he'd passed the night before. He needed food and he didn't trust the stuff on offer at Free Robots. The store sold the usual necessities — food bricks and energy drinks, cheap beer and water. Dex picked up a five pack of bricks which were reasonably inexpensive and a small bottle of water which more than doubled the cost of his purchases. With this heat, though, Dex couldn't afford not to get the extra liquid.

He ate one of the food bricks en route to Free Robots and he drank half the water, too. By the time he reached the nondescript building, he felt almost as good as if he actually had taken a nap instead of talking to Annabelle. He pulled open the door and then walked into the café. He had guessed right — where there earlier had been maybe a dozen people in the large group, now there were twice or three times that number.

They had more or less taken over the cafe, though there were still a handful of free tables. The music was louder, perhaps to compensate for the increased din from the large group of talking, laughing people. Dex headed for the bar and decided to splurge by ordering a double dark rum and real ginger beer from the touchpad. He figured that the amount of money he was saving Ivy by staying in a dive like El Presidente more than offset the price of an expensive drink. The robotic arm mixed his drink and presented it to him in record time. Dex took a sip and was instantly transported back in time.

The first taste of the smooth sweetness of the rum immediately reminded him of the old days with Maks, then the spicy aftertaste of the ginger beer almost burned his tongue and the feeling of almost literally being transported in time intensified. He hadn't tasted that sweet, spicy concoction since the night Maks left. Dex chalked up the pinpricks he felt starting in his nose and climbing up to his eyes to the heat of the drink, though that was really only part of it. He took his glass to one of the empty tables and nursed the first half of it while watching the large group and fighting his own memories.

He pulled up the images of Ljundberg and Bish that Annabelle had sent him and scanned the room. He found Bish easily, at the centre of the largest grouping, dominating conversation. He couldn't see Ljundberg anywhere, though. There were a few people who were behind the others and he couldn't really make them out. He ran the magnification program and this time was prepared for the vertigo it created. As he looked closer at the group, he became more convinced than ever that Ljundberg just wasn't there.

He reset his vision and blinked a few times to readjust. He pinged Annabelle, asking if Ljundberg had turned up online yet. She answered almost immediately that he had not, but that his ID chip had registered again at the same store Dex had been in earlier. Dex asked when that was and she told him it was less than a half hour earlier. Dex abruptly thanked her and stood, getting ready to go out and look for Ljundberg. Just as he turned toward the door, it opened and Ljundberg himself walked in.

• • •

He was shorter than Dex expected him to be; the image Annabelle had given him hadn't shown him in context and Dex still had the memory of his avatar from Marionette City in his mind. Ljundberg was one of those people who took the opportunity of making a new image for himself seriously. He could only have been more the opposite of his avatar had he been female. He had light coloured hair that was closely cropped to his skull, no facial hair of any kind and he was fashionably soft around the middle.

He walked into the Free Robots and paused a moment at the door to let his eyes adjust. He looked around, seeming to scan the large group, as if looking for a particular person. His eyes locked on someone and he made a bee line over to one of the smaller groups. It wasn't Stella Bish's table, but Dex was pretty sure it was a group of Cleansers.

Dex let Ljundberg greet the group, get a seat and a drink. He watched from a distance as the man talked earnestly with the others. Dex remembered that his conversation with Ljundberg had easily devolved into armchair philosophizing and he imagined that Ljundberg could happily talk up a storm with this group as well. He couldn't hear their conversation from his vantage point, but he guessed it would be boring and intense.

After about half an hour of watching and waiting and the last half of his drink, Dex decided it was time. He had pinged Annabelle and was streaming the video feed that he was recording so she could follow the action. They also opened a voice channel so she could talk to him if she came up with something. Dex subvocalized, "Here goes nothing," and walked over to the table where Ljundberg was sitting.

"Excuse me," Dex said, addressing the group, "I'm looking for Sterling Ljundberg." Ljundberg turned to him, looking surprised, but answering immediately.

"Yes," he said, "that's me. Do I know you?"

"We've spoken," Dex said. "Andersson Dexter." Ljundberg's expression was blank for a moment, then he frowned slightly, trying to remember if and where he'd heard the name before.

"Mr. Dexter..." Ljundberg murmured the name, then his eyes popped open and he said, "The investigator. About Reuben, yes, I remember, now." His expression went from being pleased at remembering to worried in an instant. "What are you doing here, Mr. Dexter?" "Looking for you, Mr. Ljundberg."

"Looking for me?" the man repeated, sounding confused. One of the other people at the table, a plain looking woman, spoke up at this point.

"Sterling," she said, her voice nasally and slightly whiny-sounding. "What's going on? Who is this man?"

Dex heard Annabelle's voice in his ear say, "And who are you honey?"

Ljundberg turned to the woman and said, "Don't worry, Marta, it's nothing." Turning back to Dex, he said, "Maybe we should talk privately?" He stood and indicated a table in the corner. Dex nodded, as Annabelle said she'd start looking up the woman and the two men walked away from the now silent group. Dex stopped at the bar.

"Drink?" he asked Ljundberg as he entered an order for a regular rum and gingapop. The other man shook his head and Dex picked up his cool glass, then gestured for Ljundberg to lead the way. He followed the man to a table in a quiet corner. They sat and

Dex noticed that the other man's hands were shaking slightly. Even though the café was nicely climate controlled, small beads of perspiration were appearing at Ljundberg's hairline.

"You're a tough fellow to find, Mr. Ljundberg," Dex said.

"And you just happened to be in the neighbourhood, Mr. Dexter?" Ljundberg's hands were now hidden under the table, but his voice betrayed the shaking they were certainly still doing.

"I can't say that I was," Dex answered, "though this place is almost worth the train ride." Dex took a sip of his drink and slowly moved the glass across the table, making patterns with the condensation. Annabelle told him that she got an ID on Marta — she was a clerk at the same firm as Ljundberg. There was nothing particularly interesting about her other than that she'd last been online the same time as Ljundberg.

"I'm guessing lovers," Annabelle said. Dex subvocalized his thanks and he waited for Ljundberg to fill the uncomfortable silence. He didn't wait long.

"I don't understand," Ljundberg said. "Why are you here? I don't know anything about what happened to Reuben and you didn't need to come all the way here to hear me tell you that again. Besides, I'll be online again in a couple of days."

"I didn't know that," Dex said. "All I knew is that you were missing and your name popped up again in my investigations. It all seemed rather... implausible."

"I don't understand," Ljundberg repeated. "My name... what do you mean?"

Dex wasn't ready to lay his cards on the table quite yet, so he decided to try a different approach. "This thing you all are doing," he gestured at the other patrons in the café. "The Offline Cleanse, is that right?" Ljundberg nodded. "What's it all about? Are you a bunch of weirdo tech haters who want to destroy the 'nets or what?"

Ljundberg laughed nervously, seeming to be more comfortable now that he had a question to answer. "Not at all, Mr. Dexter. We think technology is good and important and we use the 'nets just the same as everyone else. We're not trying to undo the gains we've made through technology. We just think that the 'nets aren't a substitute for the real world."

"Hmm," Dex said, looking thoughtful. "So what then, I wonder, must you make of people who exist only online? Are they not real people, to you? Or even worse — abominations to be destroyed?" Dex paused for a beat. "Is that why you killed Reuben Cobalt?"

# TWENTY-ONE

IT SEEMED AS if all the blood drained from Ljundberg's face. Dex thought it was possible the man was about to faint and wondered what he would do about it if he did pass out. Annabelle's voice sounded loudly in his ears, saying, "God damn it Dex, how about some subtlety?"

"Just let me play it my way, okay," he subvocalized back. Unaware of their conversation, Ljundberg opened his mouth as if to say something, but the only sound that came out was a strangled, high pitched moan. Dex waited for Ljundberg to regain his composure, keeping his eyes on the man. He'd thought there was a chance that Ljundberg would try to make a break for it, so he'd positioned himself between the other man and the door. Running seemed to be the last thing on Ljundberg's mind, though — he was more focussed on appearing indignant and foaming at the mouth.

Finally, he appeared to get control of himself and in a shocked tone of voice said, "I cannot believe you would accuse me of that." Dex continued with the silent treatment and Ljundberg rose to the bait. "I mean, Reuben was my friend. He was kind and harmless and so what if he was a multi? It's no crime."

"Should it be?" Dex asked.

"What?" Ljundberg said, his voice rising, as he fell back in his chair like he were somehow deflated. "No, of course not. That's ridiculous. I don't particularly think it's a healthy life choice, but it's not for me to say. I don't even understand what you're talking about."

"Would you still have been friends with Reuben if you had known he was a multi?" Dex asked, trying to draw the other man out.

"Sure," Ljundberg said, shrugging his shoulders and sounding anything but sure. "I don't see why not. I mean, we were friends because we liked to talk to each other, we shared ideas — that doesn't change just because you use one name or another. It's just a name, it doesn't mean anything."

"But it's not the same, is it?" Dex asked. "I mean, Reuben is dead, but the mind who thought those ideas is still alive. After all, it's just a name, right? It doesn't mean anything."

"That is not what I meant," Ljundberg's voice was rising in pitch and he leaned in across the table. Dex could smell the sour tang of sweat coming off the smaller man's body. "You're twisting what I say; trying to put words in my mouth. I don't think those things — I didn't do it."

"Do what?"

"You know," Ljundberg's voice rose higher. "What you're accusing me of. Of... ending... Reuben's..."

"Of killing Reuben Cobalt."

"Yeah, that."

Dex smacked his hand hard on the table between them and all other conversations in the café abruptly stopped. Annabelle gasped and Ljundberg looked like he was going to wet his pants. "For christ's sakes, you can't even say it. 'Killed.' 'Dead'. Reuben Cobalt — your friend — is dead and you can't even say it."

"He's not dead!" Ljundberg shouted, almost in tears. "He can't be. He was never alive."

• • •

That was when Ljundberg broke down. He started blubbering, tears like water raining down his face, bubbles of snot appearing at his nose. Dex had to look away, while the other people in the room now openly stared at the two men. Ljundberg's co-worker, Marta, stormed over to the table and began accusing Dex of harassment and assault and anything else she could come up with. Dex wished he'd been packing some of his old goon squad equipment — a short blast of Seda-spray would have shut her up pretty quick.

As Marta tried to decide whether to continue berating Dex or comfort Ljundberg, another figure appeared at the table. "Mr. Dexter, I presume," she said, a slight smile playing at her lips. Dex heard Annabelle say, "Well, look who decided to wade in to the fray."

Stella Bish, unlike Ljundberg, looked more or less like her avatar in Marionette City. She was wearing ordinary clothes, but the face and hair were a pretty close match. She stood at the phalanx of a group of people, though she appeared to be amused where the rest were variously angry or perplexed.

"Stella Bish," Dex said, ignoring Ljundberg to stand and face her. "The undisputed reigning monarch of independent contractors on the 'nets. How is it, I have to ask myself, that someone so intrinsically tied to the 'nets would be found here," he gestured at the group within the small bar, "with these... meat lovers." Dex had hoped to get a reaction by using such a vulgar term and by the sound of the crowd he could tell that many of the other people in the room were offended. Bish, however, merely smiled her maddeningly serene smile.

"That's business," she said, simply. "One of the few things the 'nets are good for. I work to live, Mr. Dexter, not the other way around. And this," she aped his previous gesture, "is living."

"Don't make me puke," Annabelle said.

"Shut up," Dex subvocalized, but aloud asked, "And how do your friends here feel about your work," nodding toward the other people in the room. "Are they as comfortable with your involvement in the 'nets?"

She laughed. "I would imagine so. Many of them work for me. Not to mention that I invented the Offline Cleanse. It's a little hard to question my commitment to my own ideals."

• • •

After a brief chat with her people, including a short but firm conversation with Marta, Bish managed to get a table for herself, Dex and Ljundberg where the rest of the room wasn't eavesdropping on every word. "Now I don't know anything about this situation that I haven't already told you," Bish started out with a disclaimer, "but I can be fairly sure that no one I'm involved with here killed Reuben Cobalt for ideological reasons. We do not advocate hate, we're not even opposed to the idea of multiple identities, unlike many other groups out there. We are a positive force," she said, sounding less like a marketing shill than Dex would have thought. "We aim to encourage increased interaction in this, the real world."

"You can vouch for all the members of your little flock?" Dex asked, not bothering to conceal his patronizing attitude. "You can be sure of what they did or did not do in the name of these beliefs?"

Bish smiled that smile that drove Dex crazy, the one that made him think she was playing a game with him. "Of course not, Mr. Dexter," she said. "I don't know anyone else's mind. I do know that I've heard no one talk about such things and we don't condone violence or harassment of any kind. We are in favour of creating positive change; we're not destructive."

"So you keep saying," Dex said, "and yet here I am. Sitting before the two of you, whose names keep coming up in a murder investigation. It seems strangely coincidental that a friend of the deceased is a part of a group that was started by the deceased's former employer and now is in line for the deceased's very lucrative former position with said employer. If it smells like shit, I have to wonder why everyone says it's perfume."

"Jesus, Dex," Annabelle's voice said, "could you be more bizarre?"

"Shut up, already," he repeated silently, hoping that an equal mixture of frustration and fraternity was in the translated voice. "I have a plan." At this stage, Ljundberg finally seemed to pay attention again. Until then, he had sat, almost motionless, tears, spit and snot slowly drying on his face.

"You think I..." he made a show of emphasizing the word, "killed... Reuben for his job?" He made a face that seemed to Dex to genuinely indicate revulsion at the idea. "A fucking job? That's... That's... pathetic," he finally got the last word out. "How pitiful do you think I am?"

To what Dex imagined was her horror, Annabelle said, "You don't want to know, pal" at the exact same moment that Bish smiled and turned to Ljundberg saying, "You probably don't really want Mr. Dexter to answer that question, Sterling." Dex wasn't sure, but he thought he heard Annabelle whisper, "Bitch."

"Reuben was well respected online," Dex said to Ljundberg,

softly, sounding almost like a friend. "His opinion was valued on the boards and his economic value was undeniable. Isn't that right?" He turned toward Bish, who nodded her agreement. "I can see how living in his shadow might have been hard. He had all those things you wanted — the prestige, the money — and he wasn't even a real person. It just doesn't seem fair, does it?"

"Nice one," Annabelle said, but Ljundberg said nothing. He simply started at Dex with fury in his face. This time it seemed like Ljundberg was using Dex's silent tactic, as he slowly stood without speaking. He looked down at Dex, his nose curling in distaste, then spat directly into Dex's face, a sticky sour blob hitting his left cheek and trickling down to his chin.

"Fuck you," Ljundberg said and turned away from the table. He walked to the door and out of the café. His strident friend Marta, who had been watching the proceedings with great interest, stood and fixed Dex with what he presumed was intended to be a withering look, before following Ljundberg out the door.

• • •

By now, Dex was probably the most unpopular guy the Free Robots had ever seen and once Ljundberg had stormed off, he couldn't think of any good reason to stay. He made arrangements with Stella Bish to talk to her again the next day and Annabelle agreed to track her movements as well as Ljundberg's over the course of the night.

Dex had wiped his face off with the sleeve of his shirt and as he walked back to his hotel the wet spot rubbed against his skin. It was disturbing, though Dex had certainly dealt with worse when he was on the streets with the goon squad. Not to mention that there were some parties he'd gone to in the Maks days where things not too dissimilar were done for enjoyment.

Stella Bish's talk about the people who followed the Offline Cleanse was mostly propaganda bullshit, just as Annabelle had said. But Dex had to admit that it was the kind of bullshit that appealed to him. He'd never felt comfortable socializing online and as his non-relationship with Annabelle proved, in some ways he was even more of a freak than these people with their weekends off. He knew he had no right to judge them and he actually didn't. It was what it was and if Ljundberg or any of the others killed Reuben for some fucked up ideology, that was madness, but the rest of it was all pretty much fine by him. Maybe even a little more than fine, if he was honest with himself.

Back at the hotel, he stripped and stood under the brief spray in the lav. After he was dried off, he lay on the bed, wishing he had brought another change of clothes. One set was starting to become crusty with sweat and the other was covered in Ljundberg's loogies. Not an ideal situation.

It was getting late and the excitement of the night had worn him out. He drank some of his water and ate another food brick. As Dex lay on the bed, his thoughts drifted to Ljundberg's reaction. It was so extreme, so visceral, so physical. It reminded Dex of himself as a younger man — not the reactions themselves, but the emotions they betrayed. Disbelief, fear, hurt, betrayal — all those feelings that lay dormant in him all the time, that he only let out at night, with the booze and the videos.

Dex paged over to his viewer, scanned his files and started up a video. He could feel the dreaded pinpricks in his eyes, but he closed his eyelids until the moment passed. He wished he had a bottle, but he watched the ending of his final night with Maks sober. He replayed it over and over again, watching for a good couple of hours before he finally fell asleep.

# TWENTY-TWO

ANNABELLE WOKE DEX early the next day. He had set his system to wake him for her call and he was well asleep when the chiming noise in his head roused him. He gave himself five minutes for the lav and a swig of Flying Fish, then he returned Annabelle's ping. "What do you have for me?" he said, a rasp in his voice.

"Jeez, Dex," she said, "you sound like shit."

"Truth in advertising," he said, "that's all. So, why'd you wake me up?"

"Mostly I just wanted to hear your sexy voice," she said and Dex answered with a genuinely amused short laugh. He was surprised at their now easy banter, but after that awful night at the restaurant, it was as if they now shared some kind of secret. It was strange, but Dex wasn't about to argue.

"You should have told me earlier," he said. "I could have left a recording and slept in."

Annabelle laughed and said, "Unfortunately, there's more. I think Ljundberg's on the move."

"I'm not overly surprised," Dex said. "He was pretty fucked up last night. I'm not going to get excited about it, though."

"You don't think he's going to disappear?"

"The guy has to eat, right?"

"I don't get it," Annabelle said.

"Well," Dex stretched and sniffed at his clothes. He wrinkled his nose and continued, "You can track him by his chip, right?

"Yeah, so?"

"So, he stops for food or water and we know where he is." Dex put on his less nasty clothes and made a note to check at the hotel's concierge for laundry services. "And better yet, he needs to work to pay for it. So he'll be online again soon enough, I'm sure. He's not going anywhere — there's nowhere to go."

"You seem really cool about this," Annabelle said.

"Well," Dex said, "truth be told, if Ljundberg did it, whatever his motivation, it was personal. It was about Reuben. He's no threat to anyone else, really. So, there's no rush in finding him. Besides, he seems like the kind of guy where letting him stew will make him more likely to give it up later."

"So, what's the plan now?"

"I've got a meeting with Bish," Dex said, "and I've put on my nicest outfit to wow her with."

"I'm sure she'll be all over you with that physical world bullshit of hers," Annabelle said, real venom in her voice now. "You watch it, Dex. She's a suspect, remember. Don't get sucked in by her. Her and her god damn body."

Dex was surprised by Annabelle's vitriol. "Uh, Annabelle," Dex said carefully, "I'm not going to fuck her. I know she's a suspect and I'm going to find out what she knows. Sure, we share certain... preferences, but that doesn't mean I even like her, let alone that I'm going to fall under her thrall or something. I am a pro, you know."

"I'm sorry, Dex." He could hear real sadness in her voice. "It's just... hard, you know?"

"Kind of," he said, not really understanding at all. There was silence for a moment, then Dex heard Annabelle take a deep breath.

"Look, remember that night we went out to dinner, in Marionette City?"

"With excruciating clarity," he answered.

"Exactly," she said. "You hated that. I know. I understood perfectly. Because that's exactly how I feel outside of Marionette City. In the... embodied world."

"Oh." Dex didn't know what to say.

"Yeah." Annabelle was quiet and Dex wondered if she'd muted her input. Soon enough she continued, though. "So it's kind of hard for me, knowing... what you like and knowing that it's what she likes... and knowing that I don't..."

"Aw, honey," Dex trailed off, not knowing how to say what he wanted to. Instead, he sent Annabelle a link to Marionette City. They met at Monte's. Dex walked toward Annabelle's avatar and had his avatar put its arms around her. He even felt something for a moment, though it was more like regret that this moment wasn't real than any kind of human connection and that made him feel even more sad.

"I'm sorry things are so fucked up," he said aloud, the voice connections still live.

"Me too," she said.

Dex had his avatar pull back from Annabelle's and he smiled. He wondered if he looked sad. "Aren't we a pair," he said, hoping his voice made up for any deficiencies his avatar projected. She smiled back at him and stepped back.

"Thank you for this," she said. "Really. You don't know how much it means."

He smiled and said nothing. Then, after a moment, he said, "I have to go," his avatar not moving.

"I know," Annabelle said. "Go get 'em." She punched him lightly on the shoulder and linked out of Marionette City, cutting the voice connection at the same time. Dex linked out as well, but had to wait a moment before he was able to walk out his hotel room door.

• • •

Dex was meeting Stella Bish at the Free Robots and he walked out of El Presidente then headed up the road. The weather was still hot and humid, but Dex was starting to become accustomed to it. The growing warmth over Dex's body that had previously seemed suffocating he now found comforting, like a blanket. He could see how people might want to move here — more sunlight, less rain and natural warmth. Two days seemed a bit quick to be going native, though — maybe it was just lack of sleep.

He pushed open the main door of the building and stepped into the vestibule. He checked the time at the lower right corner of his display and saw that he was a few minutes early. He hoped that he would be the first to arrive and be able to get a table and set the scene. He opened the door to Free Robots and was disappointed to see Bish at one of the booths, surrounded by a coterie of her supporters.

Dex walked up to the bar and ordered a coffee from the touchpad. It was a little early for a drink and he wanted to be alert for his talk with Bish. The metal arm poured his coffee and set the cup in front of him. Dex took it and walked to a small table for two on the far side of the room. He waited for Bish to come to him. It took longer than he would have liked, but she eventually walked over to his table.

She sat across from him and crossed her hands on front of her on the table, like a proper schoolgirl of years gone by. "You wanted to see me again," she said, that smile playing at the corner of her lips.

"I need to know more about this Offline Cleanse of yours," Dex said, especially conscious of the woman's charms. "And Sterling Ljundberg. What can you tell me about him?"

Bish unclasped her hands and leaning back in her chair and crossing her legs, she began to inspect her well-groomed fingernails. Dex noticed, for the first time, that the nails were imbued with some kind of pattern. It looked like one of the holographic colours B&B's cosmetics department sold. "I met him here," she said. "A few days ago. I don't think I'm really going to be helpful, Mr. Dexter. I didn't even know he was on my list of potentials."

"That seems unlikely," Dex said.

"I agree," Bish said, looking him in the eye, "but there it is. Besides, just because his name doesn't mean a lot to me doesn't make it a great coincidence. Plenty of the people who want to work for me are already Cleansers, or they learn about it because they want to work for me. It's not a big secret, you know."

"It's not exactly advertised on your storefront, either," Dex countered.

"True," Bish said, "but the word is out that I'm building living quarters in Europa and it doesn't take a mathematical genius to put two and two together." She was silent, watching Dex closely. He hoped that the dawning realization didn't show on his face.

"A physical world community is a pretty big step," Dex said. "You'll have to really trust your people."

"What do you mean?" she asked, looking genuinely puzzled.

"Well," Dex said, "housing that's not tied to employment is at a premium and while your staff are sort of your employees, I assume places at your building won't be meted out the usual way." She nodded her agreement and Dex continued. "So, there's a good chance people will say they agree to the idea of the Cleanse just to get a room."

"So?" she asked.

"Well, how is that building a new kind of community?"

"I think there's a wonderful and necessary thing about a community focussed around the physical world, Mr. Dexter," she said, "and I don't think it matters what people think when they first come in. So long as we are truly there — that we have activities and there is a real community, people will want to participate. We are social animals — it's what people do."

Dex thought of Annabelle. "I wouldn't be so sure," he said.

"It's a chance I'm willing to take," she answered.

Dex paused for a moment to run back the audio recording of the conversation. He caught the point where the topic had shifted and returned to his earlier point. "So, you say you met Sterling Ljundberg just a few days ago? When exactly was that?"

Bish adjusted to the abrupt shift in topics easily. "Two days ago. A local group of Cleansers have been meeting here when we are on retreat."

"Retreat?"

"That's what we call those days off, the days spent offline and in person."

"Okay," Dex said. "So you met Ljundberg two days ago…"

"Yes," she said. "He was here, I was here, we met and we talked. I didn't even recognize his name from the staff list. He mentioned it and I supposed he was trying to curry favour, increase his ranking or something. It happens sometimes at these events."

"Does it work?" Dex asked.

Bish smiled and leaned slightly toward him. "Sometimes it does," she said. "I have to admit that I find meeting people in the physical world makes me feel more comfortable with them — I tend to trust them more. So yes, meeting potential associates here can make a difference to to their chances."

"And Ljundberg?"

"Well, that's interesting," she said. "I'm not sure about him now. I was going to hire him yesterday, but today…"

"Suspicion of murder puts a pall on the trust level, does it?"

"Actually, no," Bish answered. "Well, that's not why. It was his reaction. A bit too hotheaded for me. But we'll see. My mind isn't made up yet." Dex was silent and Bish looked him directly in the eyes. "Is yours?"

Dex shifted in his seat and thought. Like he usually did when he didn't know how to respond to a question, he opted for honesty. "No," he said, "I don't think it is. But you never really know about a person. All you have are what they tell you and what you see for yourself."

"Exactly my point, Mr. Dexter," she said. "There is so little we can ever know about each other and when we waste all that time interacting virtually, we miss an entire level on which we can communicate. It's such a shame, don't you think?" She looked a Dex expectantly, as if she had asked the most important question of their conversation.

Dex thought for a moment. He understood her point of view so well and yet he found her personally to be utterly disturbing. Again, he opted for the truth.

"What I think doesn't matter." He rose from the table and walked out the door.

# TWENTY-THREE

DEX LEFT FREE Robots and as he walked down the street he messaged El Presidente and canceled his room. He settled the tab and copied the invoice to Ivy for her records. He continued down the street and stopped in at the store on the corner for another one of those extremely expensive bottles of water. While he wandered the aisles of the store, he booked his return train ticket. He would have a few hours before the overnighter ran, but he was happy to hang out at the train station. As much as he might like the physical world, he decided he'd had enough of the people here in Guadalajara.

Since he had time, Dex decided to walk to the train station. It was only a few klicks and the map he'd originally used on his way into town would show him the way. It was late in the day now and the lower humidity and heat made for a comfortable walk. Once he found his stride, he pinged Annabelle. She answered and opened a voice channel.

"So, what's the good news?" she asked, her voice light.

"Hrmph," Dex grunted. "I guess the good news is that I'm on my way to the train station."

"You're done with being a world traveler?"

"For now," Dex answered. "There isn't anything keeping me here and I have to go back to work day after tomorrow."

"You didn't get anywhere with Bish?" Annabelle asked, her voice hardening a little. Dex grunted again and sent a copy of the audio track from his recording of the meeting.

"She doesn't strike me as dangerous," he said. "Crazy, maybe, but not dangerous."

"I'm not sure you're seeing the situation clearly," Annabelle said and Dex sighed aloud.

"I know you think she's up to no good," he said, patiently, "and you may be right, but I just don't think she cares enough about any one person to be bothered with killing someone."

"Hrmph." It was Annabelle's turn to resort to sound effects as communication.

"What about Ljundberg?" Dex asked.

"I'm pretty sure he's holed up in his apartment in Guadalajara," Annabelle said. "I checked his employment records and he has a place in town. He's trying to be sneaky, since he hasn't logged on yet and he bypassed the door lock mechanism by using a mechanical key, but I'll give you 20 to one odds that he's there."

"Oh?" Dex indicated that she should continue.

"He's sending his little friend Marta out for provisions," Annabelle said, sounding pleased with herself. "I've tracked her ID chip at a store near there a couple of times now. You'd think they'd be smarter than that, but there it is."

"There it is," Dex said, with a little less glee than Annabelle had expressed when she uttered the words. According to the map super-imposing itself over the vision on his right eye, Dex was more or less following the local train's route to the station. He was a block or two west of the tracks and he couldn't see or hear the train, but he knew he was on the right path. Even walking he would have more time at the station than he needed, but he was sure he could catch up on some work while waiting.

As if she could read his mind, Annabelle said, "I had an idea last night, but it's going to take some time and I don't know if it will even be useful..."

"What is it?"

"Well," she said, "you mentioned that you have a list of all of Bish's staff members, right?"

"Yeah."

"Well, maybe someone ought to go through the whole thing and see if any other names pop up. You know, just in case?"

Dex rubbed his face with his hands and found that his head was covered in a fine shimmer of sweat. "Yeah, that's not a bad idea," he said, reluctantly. "And I've got time, too. I'll do it."

"It just seems like we ought to be covering our bases, you know?" she said, as if she still had to convince him.

"I know," he said. "I'll do it. It's a good idea. So, 1 while I'm reading names until my eyeballs bleed, what exciting plans do you have for yourself?"

"Well," she said, "I'll have one eye watching Bish and Ljundberg's movements in the meat... I mean physical world and I figured I'd see if I can trace their online movements for the past week or so. See if I can tie either of them to the actual spot of Reuben's murder. Or maybe to the attack on you."

"Good thinking," Dex said. "Now, I'm going to end this call before I pass out. I'm walking to the train station and this talking and walking at the same time is making my head spin."

"You're doing what?" Her voice was almost shrill. "Why can't you just take a train like a normal human being?"

"I was bored," Dex said. "And besides, I've never been to Mexico before. I ought to at least see the place before I leave."

"You are so twentieth century," she said, laughing. "Catch you later." She broke the connection and Dex panted a little, trying to get his breath back.

• • •

Dex continued the rest of the journey to the train station without focussing on anything else, just the map and the sidewalk and the scenery. He decided that Guadalajara wasn't that great after all, it was just a warmer, damper version of every other city he'd been to.

He had an hour and a half to wait before the train north would be leaving, so Dex found a spot on the cramped and uncomfortable seats in the waiting area. The station was not very busy, so he stuck his small bag at the end of one of the benches, then using it as a pillow, stretched out longwise on the bench. It was no lap of luxury, but he thought that his various body parts might not fall asleep in the ninety minutes he had to kill.

Dex paged over to the file he'd gotten from Uri Farone and started reading.

Aadams, Adelman, Ariane, Avalon, Barnett, Basri, Bellinger, Bischoff, Bosun, Buttle, Cameron... Dex scanned the names, but by the time he got to the Gs his eyes were already starting to glaze over. He focussed harder and slowed down, checking the list more closely, but nothing jumped out at him. The list wasn't up to date — his eyes had stumbled over Cobalt — but even so there wasn't anything that struck him.

He found the link Farone had given him to the list of people who were next in line for work. There were fewer names there, but only Ljundberg's name rang any bells for Dex. He was starting to think that he was looking in all the wrong places. Maybe it was just a coincidence that Ljundberg was a pal of Reuben's and was going after the former multi's job. Maybe it had nothing to do with Reuben's work. The trouble was that Reuben didn't seem to have any enemies and there was no doubt that this was no random act. The code that caused Reuben to destroy himself was coded specifically to fulfill that very particular job and then destroy itself along with its victim. If this had been about "cleansing Marionette City of multis," the code would have been, at least potentially, self-replicating. As it was, the code was carefully written to destroy itself.

So, Dex figured, this had to be someone who cared about not unleashing a multi killing virus on Marionette City. He thought and came to the conclusion that this one fact made it even less likely that Stella Bish was involved. Dex doubted that she had any interest in actively destroying multis, but she certainly didn't seem to care enough about anyone to specifically try to avoid any kind of collateral damage. That seemed more to be Ljundberg's style. He was emotional and this was an emotional crime. It was personal in both senses — the act was meaningful to the killer and it was about Reuben specifically. If only Dex could have gotten through to Ljundberg.

• • •

Dex spent the rest of the time at the station thinking about the case, wondering if he had taken on an unsolvable crime. Only two days earlier he had been so sure that he was on to it. He had been certain that could feel the unravelling starting and now he felt as tied up in the threads of the mystery as he had when he had first begun. He was wasting Annabelle's time on this case and he worried that if they never got a result that she would hold it against him. He wondered why that thought mattered to him. Until recently, Dex had always been perfectly happy to use other members of the Cubicle Men — that was what they were for. More like Stella Bish than he'd like to admit, Dex had seen his colleagues as resources to be used, no more and no less. But now, it seemed like something had changed. Dex wasn't sure that it was a positive change.

The chime in the station sounded and Dex rolled off the bench. He grabbed his bag and boarded the train. He found his seat and settled in. After the hard station bench, the train's seat felt like it was made of pillows. Dex debated about killing the trip with SleepingJuice's perfect oblivion, but he wasn't tired yet. His brain couldn't take thinking about the case any more and although he found that he wanted to talk to her, he didn't know what to say to Annabelle. He paged over to his video collection and opened up his viewer.

He picked a recording of a night from what he thought of as the end days — after Maks decided to move but before he actually did. They were lying on the floor of the apartment, listening to music like usual. The song was fast, with a strong and steady beat. The track was maybe ten or fifteen minutes long, the notes jumbling together but still distinct, with a rhythm that somehow drove into Dex's body, lifting and carrying him along the crests and troughs of the song. Even hearing it now, sober and with the gulf of time between himself and the moment, he felt the hypnotic effects of the music on his body.

There wasn't a lot to see in the video record. They didn't talk during the song, each lying on their separate patch of floor, eyes closed, a private journey fueled by the music. Those were the moments that were the hardest to explain and the ones that he missed the most — the memories that cut into him with a terrible burning pleasure. It was the times they didn't talk, the times they were alone but together. It was the one thing that virtuality could never even pretend to emulate. Dex knew there was a kind of intimacy in that silent, solitary experience that was shared and yet entirely personal at the same time.

He watched as the song ended and they each slowly stirred back to life. Dex saw Maks sit up, rolling his shoulders to work out the kinks they'd developed lying on the hard floor. He saw his younger self roll over and sit up, eyes blinking to get accustomed to the dim light. He saw his eyes meet Maksym's gaze and saw the other man smile. Maks had always been a pretty happy go lucky guy, but Dex thought he saw a hint of sadness on the other man's lips. They had looked at each other in silence for a moment, then Maks had nodded and his smile broadened. "Nice," he had said, the word drawn out and imbued with meaning.

Dex saw himself nod, acknowledging the shared experience of the song and its effects. He ended the video, closed his eyes and put the song on loop. It must have repeated twenty times before he shut it off as he got off the train.

# TWENTY-FOUR

DEX RODE THE local train from the station to his apartment building, shivering from a newfound aversion to the cold. He was amazed at how just a couple of days in a warm climate could change his comfort level at home. He tucked his arms in to his sides as he clung to the vertical rail on the train, trying to conserve as much warmth as possible. He went online and had his system instruct his apartment to turn on the heat and double up the water quota. He figured that he had a couple of days worth of water rations saved and he could use an extra long shower.

At his stop, he stepped off the train and a cool breeze hit him, making his body shiver. He hurried toward his building, hands tucked deep into his pockets. He opened the door and stepped onto the up lift. When he got into his apartment, he immediately shucked off his clothes and dumped the contents of his bag out. He stuffed all his dirty clothes into the autoclave and stepped into the lav, turning on the water. He stood under the weak spray and when the blower came on, he stayed under the warm air longer than he needed to. Eventually, he stepped out of the small room and put on some clean clothes.

It was late, getting close to the middle of the night, but Dex just wasn't tired. His usually well ordered routine had been broken in the last few days and now time was becoming even less relevant that it had been before. He knew he could just grab the SleepingJuice and let it work its magic, but it wasn't just that he wasn't tired. He didn't want to sleep. He pulled out the bottle of Jamaica's Best, now getting dangerously close to empty and poured a generous shot into a tumbler. He topped it off with a splash of ginger ale and sat in his comfortable chair.

The apartment had warmed nicely up by then and Dex set the controls back to normal. He dimmed the lights a little, creating a softer atmosphere that he hoped would be conducive to thinking. He logged in to the Cubicle Men's system and pulled up the case file he'd been keeping. He scanned through his notes, thinking that there must be something he had missed. He had that feeling, like a tiny itch at the base of his neck, that made him think he was missing something important. He read over his notes from the beginning of the case and noticed that Annabelle had started adding her observations as well. She really was great — Dex was sure he would never have even gotten this far without her help. It would be strange not talking to her all the time once the case was over.

When he got to the end of the file, Dex noticed that Annabelle had added some information just recently, while he was on the train from Guadalajara, in fact. Her note was somewhat cryptic, stating that her search for subjects SL and SB over the previous week was inconclusive and that online trails for both parties appeared to be unavailable. Dex had no idea what this meant, so pinged Annabelle. Of course, since it was the middle of the night, there was no response.

Dex sighed and took a slug of his drink. He was relying on Annabelle too much, wanting to talk to her about the case, wanting to talk to her period. He'd always worked alone — most of the Cubicle Men did — and that was the way he wanted it. No discussions, no meetings, no disagreements. So why did he feel completely and utterly lost because he couldn't talk to her?

He leaned back in the chair and started paging through the Cubicle Men's system, checking out the other cases. It was all just the usual stuff and none of it was taking Dex's mind off his own work. Instead, he found a message from Jay Shiraishi asking if Dex had any new information. It seemed the multi community were hoping for a conclusion to the case as well.

Dex sent his old pal a quick note saying little that the other man couldn't have read in the case file. Then, Dex paged out of the organization's system and over to the boards where Reuben had spent time. He ran a search for any recent mentions of Reuben Cobalt and was surprised to find a number of long and well populated threads. They all began with the announcement of Reuben's death and were full of nice thoughts about him from people who had and had not interacted with him.

It was interesting, Dex thought, how people said the nicest things about someone only once they were gone. It was as if people were usually too afraid to tell each other how they feel, but once someone is no longer there, everyone feels the need to say those things, the things they usually never even articulate to themselves, but that eat away at you when the opportunity is gone.

He read the tributes, the memories of Reuben and the words of people who wished they had known him or known him better. He wondered if Ivy had seen these threads, if she read them and what it meant to her. He finished his drink and even though he still wasn't tired, he didn't have the energy to stay awake either. He took a shot of SleepingJuice and decided to defer his problems for a few hours.

• • •

His system alarm went off in the morning and Dex awoke with a queasy feeling. It wasn't just the result of a couple of days of strong coffee, a strange bed and not enough food or sleep. It was the sick feeling of defeat, that he was never going to solve this case. Dex wasn't really an optimist, but he was ordinarily a confident man. However, this morning the sense that he was missing the key to this problem was overwhelming. He took a drink of Flying Fish and it sorted out the physical symptoms, but his mind was still unable to focus.

He was dejectedly drinking his coffee — now weak and tasteless in comparison to the brew he'd had at Free Robots — when Annabelle pinged him. Dex felt his heart rate increase and he silently chided himself for the reaction. He swallowed, cleared his throat and answered Annabelle's call.

"Hey, what's up?" he said.

"You called me, right?" she said, her voice light. "That should be my question."

"Oh, yeah," Dex said, now remembering his research from the night before. "I was reading the case notes and you added something yesterday. What was that all about?"

"Oh, that," Annabelle's voice turned serious and she sounded less than thrilled. "I have news. Or more accurately, no news."

"No news isn't good news, is it?" Dex asked.

"Not for us, it isn't," Annabelle said. "It turns out that both Sterling Ljundberg and Stella Bish were off on their little offline retreats when Reuben got killed."

"Shit."

"Shit, indeed," Annabelle said. "It doesn't prove anything — the nasty payload that killed Reuben could have been delivered by a bot, just like what happened to you. Hell, it probably was, considering that it was a bot that tried to attack you. But there's nothing in the logs that ties either of them to the event."

"Fuck," Dex said, his hand involuntarily clenched into fists. "This case is killing me. I can tell there's something I'm missing; I can just feel it. It's like I'm looking at the world around me and I can see that there's a file open on my viewer, but I just can't focus on it. It's maddening."

"I know it feels like we aren't getting anywhere," Annabelle said, her voice softening, "but I believe you'll get it. It's just a matter of time. You've got the knack, Dex. You just have to let it come."

"Thanks," Dex said, unconvinced. "I hope you're right."

"Me, too," Annabelle said and laughed. "I'm going to go and let your do your thing. I'll let you know if I find anything, okay?"

"Yeah," Dex said. "Talk to you later." He broke the connection and poured another cup of coffee. That nauseous feeling had passed into the tingly, itchy feeling again. Dex was convinced that he had seen, read or heard something that just wasn't sinking in.

He pulled up the case file and started poking through his notes again. He was hoping that he could see the information with a fresh view, but instead it was like the words were swimming before his eyes. He decided to try a different approach and put together a cross reference script. Because Dex kept recordings of every meeting or conversation, his case file was naturally divided into discrete sections of information based on when he'd recorded it. He'd made some manual links already, but there might be something else that went together. He knew that even with the script he'd have to go through the results carefully. But at least it was a different way of looking at it all.

He knew he'd have at least half an hour to kill while the script was running. Dex glared at his half full coffee cup, wondering if it would be a waste of perfectly good rum to top off the foul brown sludge with the last of the liquor. He decided it would be and dumped the coffee down the drain. There wasn't enough room in his small apartment to properly pace and he couldn't face a video, or even music now. Without even realizing what he was doing, Dex paged over to Uri Farone's storefront. He found himself looking at the options available, although he had already come close to memorizing Farone's price sheet. He wished he'd never heard of Farone's service; knowing that he could do something about his memories was, in many ways, worse than the memories themselves. As it was, he'd known for some time that he was unhealthily obsessed with his past, but he could live with that. Knowing that there was something he could do about it, that he could choose to remove the memories and therefore change his life, that meant he had to decide. He had to choose what to do.

If he removed the memories, Dex felt that it would be like he was denying his past, that part of his life that he felt was more important than anything else he'd experienced. Yet, if he chose to leave things the way they were, that meant choosing to live with the pain, choosing to be a slave to his memories. There seemed to be no way to win.

A chime sounded and Dex was saved from this debate as he saw that his script was finished. He paged over to the report that it had generated and he began to read. Mostly, the script had found connections that Dex already knew about — Ljundberg and Bish, Jay Shiraishi and Reuben, Marta and Ljundberg's day job. There were others, though, and Dex spent some time checking up on each of the items.

Even though he was specifically looking for items that had previously fallen through the cracks of his logic, he almost missed it. A name that was only ever at the periphery of the case, a person he'd only ever spoken to once and even then it was as an aside. A name that popped up so unexpectedly that he hadn't even recognized it. A name so unfamiliar that even when his script pointed it out to him he nearly let it pass by.

Renna Bellinger. Ivy's friend, who never knew about Reuben

and who had nothing to do with the case. Renna Bellinger, who was also on Stella Bish's staff list. Renna Bellinger, who was a top rated programmer with the same firm as Ivy and who worked as a contractor for Stella Bish.

Dex found his contact information for Bellinger and sent her a vague yet forceful invitation to meet with him online later that day. He pinged Annabelle and briefly told her what he'd found.

"I'm coming," Annabelle said, her voice brooking no argument.

"Not in person, you aren't," Dex said, equally forcefully.

"She doesn't need to see me," Annabelle said, "but I want to be there. You owe me that much, Dex."

Dex knew it was true. He did owe Annabelle, a lot. She had become as much a part of this investigation as he was and it was only fair that she be part of this conversation. But he didn't think he could do his job with Annabelle's voice in his ear. After much wheedling, Annabelle agreed to keep her voice connection off and to just patch into Dex's recording feed of the meeting. They spoke briefly about the plan, then Dex prepared to meet Bellinger over drinks in Marionette City.

# TWENTY-FIVE

MONTE'S, WHILE BEING Dex's first choice as an interview location, wasn't going to do. Ivy had been there several times and Dex had even met both Ivy and Bellinger there before. No, he needed a neutral location, so he asked Annabelle. She named a few spots that fulfilled all of his needs — quiet, public but out of the way locations. Dex logged into Marionette City and scouted out Annabelle's bars, finally deciding on a place called Lucky's. It was dark, with an old fashioned dark wood and burgundy leather decor. The place was small, but there would be no problem getting a table and the most important feature was that there was a back door. It meant that Annabelle could track Bellinger's movements if she tried to run.

He got there early and found a secluded table near the back. He had received a confirmation ping from Bellinger earlier and he sent her a link to the bar. He had reviewed the recording of his earlier meeting with her, but he was still unprepared for her arrival. He had been expecting the subdued redhead that he'd met at Monte's with Ivy and the others, not the silver coated creature who linked in to Lucky's.

The face of the avatar was the same, but that was about all. Where she had been ordinary and quiet before, she was shiny and glowing now. Even her hair glittered in the low lights of the bar. She scanned the room and Dex pinged her so she would more easily find her way to the table. She walked over to him and he thought that maybe strutted was a better term. She reminded him a little of the dancers that Mickey Udo had visited with Reuben. It was disconcerting.

She approached the table and the avatars shook hands. She sat across from him and Dex watched as a virtual White Russian appeared in front of her. He sipped his dark and stormy, wondering if she was getting her drink with or without the neural stims. "Mr. Dexter," she said, her voice low and even. "It's nice to see you again."

"And you, Ms. Bellinger," he answered. He studied her and saw that she kept fussing with her appearance. A hand to the hair, slight corrections to the rate of shine on her slivery skin, expecting fabric where there was none. Dex guessed that the new look was, in fact, quite new. She sipped her drink and then looked around the small bar.

"I see that your good taste in drinking establishments hasn't diminished any," she smiled.

"It's not a bad little place," Dex said, smoothly. "So, what did you want to see me about?" she asked, stirring her drink absently.

"It's about the case I'm working on that Ms. Velasquez helped me with," Dex lied. "I was hoping your could clear up a few things for me."

"Oh?" Bellinger said, the pitch of her voice rising slightly. She continued to stir her drink rhythmically.

"You're a programmer at the same firm as Ms. Velasquez, isn't that right?"

"Yes," she answered, guardedly.

"What's your specialization there?"

"I design three dimensional interactive virtual user interfaces."

"Avatars?"

"Usually," she smiled and sipped her drink. When she replaced it on the table, she began stirring it again.

"Good," Dex said. "That's exactly what I need. I was hoping you could take a look at some code for me. It's part of a case — I can't talk about that, of course — but I could really use a professional's eye on it. May I send it to you?"

Bellinger stirred her drink faster and said, "Sure." Dex pinged her system and sent her a copy of the code that his attacker had used against him, the code that had killed Reuben. He watched as she stirred her drink, then all of a sudden her avatar went completely still.

"Ms. Bellinger," he said, but there was no response. He opened up a voice channel with Annabelle, who was already in mid sentence.

"... still there, she just isn't sending any input. If you just wait, she'll come back. I think."

"Okay," he subvocalized to Annabelle, "I'm going to turn you off again. Use the emergency channel if you need to talk to me." He cut the connection and waited for Renna Bellinger to unfreeze.

• • •

It didn't take long for her avatar to start responding again, but her demeanor had changed so much it was as if she were a different person. She no longer stirred her drink incessantly, instead she completely ignored it. Rather, Bellinger focussed intensely on Dex, her head cocked slightly to the left. She seemed calmer, almost serene somehow. It threw Dex off.

"I suppose you're very proud of yourself," she said, finally, with only a hint of malice. "Catching the big bad killer." Her voice was sarcastic and Dex wondered for the first time if she might be under the influence of some drug. "What gave it away?" she asked. "Was it my coding style? Did you find something that tied me to the bot that tried to pass the code to your avatar? How did you figure it out?"

"You told me," Dex answered.

"How?" Bellinger said, her voice getting louder with equal parts curiosity and anger. "We've hardly ever even spoken. When did I say anything that could have tipped you off?"

He answered quietly, "About twenty seconds ago." She looked at him with that calm silent gaze and Dex waited for her next move.

"You didn't know," she finally said, her voice suddenly quiet. "You were just trying to find out what I knew, what I'd say. You never knew until now."

Dex shrugged. "I hate to ruin the illusion, but most of good detective work is just watching and waiting. And being at the right place at the right time to find the answer. So, now that I do know, do you want to talk about it? Tell me why you did it?"

Bellinger leaned back in her chair, a cigarette materializing between her fingers. Dex wondered if there were some kind of neural stims involved here as well. "She never even told you that I'm her wife, did she?" she asked, her voice hard with bitterness now. Dex shook his head, hoping that he was successfully concealing his surprise.

"We met through work, at one of those awful mandatory parties for all employees. They sat us together by classification and I ended up next to Ivy. We hit it off right away. Maybe it was because we were doing the same kind of work, or maybe it was that we both liked to talk about ideas — what things meant, how the world was changing, how we were a part of it all.

"We started to spend a lot of time together in Marionette City. We'd been together a couple of years when we decided to get married. I know it's an antiquated notion, but we felt like we needed something, some event to mark the occasion. It was one of the things we liked to talk about, how virtuality had created a renewed need for ritual and structure." She took a drag off of her cigarette and looked off somewhere over Dex's left shoulder. Her voice took on a wistful quality, replacing the bitter tone she'd had.

"It was such a beautiful day. We flew over the great canyon on Tropical Island, hand in hand, watching the sun go down. We were both so happy; I thought I was the luckiest person in any world, physical or virtual."

Bellinger refocussed on Dex and pinged his system. He accepted the download and opened an image of Ivy's and Bellinger's avatars, each dressed in beautiful gowns, grinning under a canopy of flowers and bells. "You both looked lovely," he said.

As if she hadn't even heard him, Bellinger continued. "It was wonderful at first. We were even happier after the wedding than before. But then Ivy started getting distant. We started to meet less often and she wasn't as interested in me, in my ideas, in my form." She ran her hands over her shimmering body. "I tried everything — leaving her alone, paying more attention to her; I even changed my avatar for her in case that was it." She began to cry, virtual tears flowing down her cheeks, and her voice fought against a sob.

"It was a long time coming," she said, "and at first I didn't notice. But she was changing and she was changing into someone who didn't want me. I had been moonlighting as a contractor with Stella

Bish and I heard about a new hot shot UI developer who'd started — some guy named Reuben Cobalt. I was impressed, so I checked him out. I never would have guessed...

"At first I thought she was in love with him. She never mentioned him, of course, but I knew the boards she read, the company she kept. Just because her name wasn't there, that didn't mean anything. She would have to know him and he was everything she would want. I was convinced that he was stealing her away from me." Her voice broke and she swallowed hard. "I didn't realize how right I truly was.

"I followed him around the 'nets and of course, I broke into the logs. I saw where he went, who he talked to, the things he likes to look at. I should have seen it long before I did. It didn't take long to have the proof and I couldn't pretend any more that I didn't know. He was her multi. He was what she wanted to become. And he didn't even know me.

"I don't know how she thought she could keep it from me," Bellinger frowned at the thought and the sob she'd been trying to stifle nearly broke through. "I'd know her code anywhere. Did she really think I wouldn't notice that it was her? I loved everything about her, of course I'd see her in his code."

She looked directly at Dex, her eyes full of tears, her chin quivering. "People change, I understand that. Of course, we all do. But we were supposed to change together." Her voice broke again, but she kept it together. "Instead, she was going to leave me and become someone else, someone entirely different. And I'd never see her again. How could I let that happen? I couldn't just let him take the woman I love away from me." The sob finally broke free and Bellinger hung her head, letting the tears flow freely.

Dex sat there a moment, watching Renna cry. Then, he carefully turned off the video stream to Annabelle and turned off his own recording. He stood and walked around the table to where the woman sat weeping. He sat down next to her and put his arms around her. "I understand," he whispered and held her, slowly rocking her, until the tears stopped.

"What is going to happen to me?" she asked once she had stopped crying.

"I don't really know," Dex said, softly. "What you did isn't technically illegal, so you don't have to worry on that front. But," he paused and lifted her chin so that she looked him in the eye. "I am going to have to tell Ivy." He expected her to start weeping again, but instead she got a stoic look on her face.

"It was only ever a matter of time," she said, resignation in her voice. "Even if she never knew what I did, she'd still leave me. I see that now. Maybe it's better this way — at least she'll see how much I love her."

Dex sighed, wondering not for the first time why so many people think that the best way to demonstrate love is by hurting themselves or others. He asked her if she needed him to call anyone for her, but she said that she would be fine. Then he left her and wrote a brief report to Ivy. He sent the report, along with a copy of the recording he'd made of most of his conversation with Renna. It was up to her how she dealt with the situation. His part was done.

# TWENTY-SIX

DEX WENT OFFLINE. His mouth was dry and his head hurt, but those were symptoms he could deal with. The dull, empty ache just above his gut was more of a problem. It was a familiar feeling, that he recognized as a twinge he usually dulled with rum. He was accustomed to it flaring up every once in a while, but he had been keeping in check until now. Renna's story was typical enough — a woman scorned — but for some reason her particular struggle hit home to Dex. He thought he could almost sense her feelings of rejection and isolation, of being left behind.

He knew it was his own memory giving him the false empathy for his client's killer, but that only made the feelings worse. He stood and walked the few paces to his small kitchen. He drank a glass of water and then filled his tumbler with half of the dregs of the Jamaica's Best. He didn't even bother with the gingapop before he drank it down, grimacing as if it were medicine. He went to the lav and when he returned to the main room, he refilled his glass with his more typical cocktail mix and went back to his chair. He still had that melancholy jangly feeling, but the edges, which had been razor raw a few moments before, now held only the dull throb of a day old wound.

He went back online to file his final case report and saw that he had several messages from Annabelle in the last half hour, all increasing in urgency and tones of panic. "Shit," he said aloud and pinged Annabelle. She answered immediately and Dex had to turn the volume down as she harangued him.

"What the fuck is going on?" she demanded, her voice rising in pitch. "All of a sudden the feed cuts out and there I am wondering what the hell is happening. Did she take a shot at you again? Are you okay?"

"Jesus," Dex muttered under his breath. "No, she didn't try for me, I'm fine. I didn't mean to worry you."

"Well, what happened to the feed, then," she asked, notes of panic still evident in her voice.

Dex debated making up some tale about the feed just cutting out, but he knew that he'd never be able to snow a pro like Annabelle. He swallowed hard. "There was just something I didn't want," he paused a moment, "something I didn't want on the record. For her sake and for the client. But everything is fine. It's over now."

"Huh," Annabelle grunted. Dex thought she was going to grill him about why there would be something he didn't want on the record, but she let it pass. "You really had me worried there," she said, her voice sounding like she was barely winning a hard-fought battle with her emotions for control. "That nut was pretty unhinged."

"I don't know if she really is a nut," Dex said.

"What?" Annabelle asked. "She put in a lot of effort to delete her honey's little side project, when they could have just had a conversation like normal people. Sounds a little nutty to me, I have to say."

"She was hurt," Dex said, quietly. "Ivy was all she ever wanted but she wasn't enough for Ivy. That's a killer feeling, kiddo. It really is."

"Oh, come on. Ivy wasn't really going anywhere," Annabelle said, incredulously. "You don't make a multi to change your life. It's just an easy way to pretend to be someone different for an hour or two. I've seen it a thousand times." Her voice had taken on a bitter tone that Dex didn't like very much. "Multis are for the dickless, Dex, for those people who just want to try on a new identity like you'd wear a new avatar or hair colour. Trust me," she said, her voice wavering slightly, "it takes more than a new name to really change your life."

"Don't I know it," Dex said, his eyes clouding over against his will. He took another slug of his drink. "But I think this was the real thing, Annabelle. I'm sure Ivy really was going to leave her old life behind."

"How can you know that?" Annabelle said, snorting.

"Bellinger certainly thought so," Dex said.

"The wife always knows, right?" Annabelle asked, sarcastically.

"In my experience, usually she does, yeah," Dex said. "Besides, Ivy told me herself that she wanted to completely change identities. You should have seen her when she realized Rueben was really gone. It was like someone stole her future away from her."

"Huh," Annabelle grunted. "I suppose it's possible," she conceded. "I'll confess that I watched your interview with her and she really did look like a little lost lamb there. But, I just don't know who to feel bad for in this one. It takes balls to stand up and do what you need to do to start a new life and a lot of eggs get broken making that omelette no matter how you play it. But you have to be willing to make those hard choices, to have those terrible conversations, or you never get free. I mean, even if Ivy was trying to come to terms with who she really is, that doesn't excuse cutting Bellinger out of her life without even saying 'see ya'." She paused and Dex wondered what she was thinking. "But, while I still don't think dusting a multi is the same as murder," she continued, "Bellinger doesn't make herself all that sympathetic with her little code bomb." She paused, as if trying to come up with a way to make it all make sense. Finally, she said, "It's a shit sandwich Dex."

"I know it is," he said, smiling mirthlessly, "but that's life."

• • •

After he got done with Annabelle, Dex logged into the Cubicle Men's system. He saw that Ivy had closed out her account with the organization, marking the transaction as successfully resolved. "That's a pretty piss poor definition of success," Dex said aloud to his empty apartment, then finished his final report, officially ending the case. After his closed out the last file, he went offline. He didn't get up from the chair, but sat looking at nothing but the four, drab grey walls around him. He swirled his drink in the glass, thinking about Ivy and Bellinger and the mess they had each made of their lives. He thought for a long time, long enough to make a casual observer wonder if he'd fallen asleep with his eyes open and his drink in his hand, until his set his glass down on the table and logged into Marionette City.

• • •

Dex felt like hell when walked into Uri Farone's storefront. Farone himself was working the shop again and he must have had a great avatar recognition program running, because he said, "Mr. Dexter, how nice to see you again. Have you decided we can do something for you after all?"

Dex closed his eyes, feeling the pinpricks start under his eyelids. "Yes," he said, "I think I have."

# TWENTY-SEVEN

THE ROOM WAS getting lighter, the weak sun coming up and brightening the place. The music had gotten slower, more dreamy and introspective as the evening progressed. By now, Maksym looked like he was fighting off sleep as he lay on the couch, his head barely nodding in time to the music. From his vantage point on the floor, Dex faced the wall and his own tiredness was making it difficult to look elsewhere. His voice sounded overly loud in the small room. "Do you want me to come with you?" he asked. "Do you need a hand on the train or anything?"

"Naw," Maks said, "it's just the one crate. Besides, you'll need to pack up, too. You'll be out of here in a few days yourself." Maks sat up and rubbing his hands over his face, said, "Andy, we've had some good times here, haven't we?"

"Yeah," Dex had said, "we have, indeed." His voice sounded tired and sad. As he stood to get a glass of water, he cleared his throat. He drew some water, drank it and poured another glass which he handed to Maks. The other man drank the whole glass in one swallow, then smiled at Dex as he gave back him the empty glass. "You should go soon," Dex said.

"Yeah," Maks said, standing up. He ran his hands over his wrinkled clothes and through his messy blonde hair, though it didn't improve their appearance any. He looked uncomfortable, like he was trying to say something but was having trouble finding the right words. "It's not you, you know," he said, finally, looking Dex in the eye. "It's just that things change. I changed. I want a different life now, that's all."

"I know," Dex said, blinking his wet eyes a few times.

"I wish everything would be the same for you once I'm gone, but it won't," Maks said, sadly. "It's a different world out there and I want to be a part of it now. I know it wasn't supposed to end this way, but I can't pretend that this is enough for me anymore."

"I know," Dex repeated. "I just wish it were."

Maks smiled and moved closer to Dex. He put his arms around the man, they embraced. "You can't hold on to people forever," Maks said, softly. "We're all in motion, constantly. Sometimes, when we're lucky, we're moving in the same direction at the same time. But, if you try to hang on, all you do is grab on to thin air. It's no good." He broke the embrace and Dex could see a tear brimming in Maksym's eye. "You have to find your own way, same as I did. But you'll be fine — you've always been the strong one, anyway." He smiled and picked up his crate. "Take care, Andy."

"You too, Maks," Dex said, as Maks walked into to hall and closed the door behind him. Dex could hear footsteps as Maks walked down the hall, footsteps that got quieter until the video went silent.

• • •

The video still made Dex feel sad every time he watched it, but those times had become fewer and further between. The first year after Maks moved out and Dex had started working at a firm he had watched the old videos almost every night. But now he couldn't even remember the last time he'd pulled out one of the recordings. He wondered what it was about today that made him want to relive those old memories. It was probably the case he'd just finished — poor Renna Bellinger and her inability to let go. It must have been hard for her. Not that it excused anything, but Dex found that he had a strong sense of sympathy for the woman that he couldn't quite understand.

He shut down the viewer and poured a glass of gingapop. He pulled out the brand new bottle of Jamaica's Best he'd picked up on the way home from work and broke the seal on the cap. He splashed a bit of the sweet dark liquor into his soda and swirled the mixture around in the glass. He sat back down in his comfortable chair and pinged Annabelle.

To his surprise, they had kept in touch in the three days since the case ended. They'd spoken in some way every day since then and while Dex didn't see himself getting over his discomfort at being together only virtually, he was enjoying their growing friendship.

Annabelle answered the ping and opened a voice channel. "Hey, there," she said, her voice light as usual. "How's it going?"

"I'm good," Dex said. "Just enjoying a tasty beverage and taking a breather after a short day at work." Annabelle laughed and Dex grinned. "Between no new cases to pick up and these short days, I almost feel like I'm on holiday. It is kind of nice having a few days off, though. I know I'll get bored soon enough, but right now I'm really liking having nothing to do in the evenings."

"Must be nice," Annabelle said. "My work is pretty much never done. I've got an intellectual property theft case of my own on the go and there are a few people who call on me every once and again for technical help."

"It's tough being popular," Dex said.

"Don't I know it," Annabelle agreed, laughing. "The good news is that I decided to take my two weeks' vacation from the day job, so I've got a nice bit of spare time to play with."

"Good for you," Dex said. "What are you planning to do with it?"

"I though I'd go visit a friend," Annabelle said and at that moment Dex heard a banging sound coming from his hallway. He got up and walked to the door. The noise sounded again and he realized that someone was knocking on the door. He tentatively opened it. A man stood there, smiling shyly. He was medium height, medium build, face full of metal — extremely ordinary-looking. He blinked a few times and said in a low, quiet voice, "Hey, Dex."

Simultaneously in his ear, Dex heard Annabelle's light voice say the same words. He blinked a few times, opened his mouth, but nothing came out.

"Yeah, it's me," the man before him and the voice in his head said, at the same time. "I know I'm probably not what you expected.... but can I come in, anyway?" Dex simply nodded and moved back from the door in order to let the man in.

• • •

They sat at the table across from each other, each drinking a strong cocktail which Dex expertly mixed. "I officially changed my gender," Annabelle said, having trouble meeting Dex's eyes, "almost ten years ago now. I never got around to doing anything with the meat." She indicated her male body sitting across from Dex. "It just never seemed to matter."

Dex said nothing for a moment, trying to take it all in. "It's none of my business," he said finally, "but is this maybe why you have such trouble in the physical world?

Annabelle shook her head. "No. I was like that before," she said. "That's why I never bothered with changing my body. It really didn't matter to me. Not to mention that the procedure is very expensive. And not without a fair amount of discomfort, I'm told."

"I'm not asking you to do it," Dex said and smiled to take the edge of his words. Annabelle smiled back and their eyes met for a brief moment. Dex sighed and took a large sip of his drink. "It's true that I want a real body to touch, but I've never been too particular about the specifics of said body."

Dex felt his face flush as he waited for Annabelle's response. "You are a very strange man," she said, finally and Dex saw a smile creep over her face.

"Look who's talking, kiddo," he said, grinning back. "It must feel so weird for you to be here."

"You have no idea," Annabelle laughed and Dex could hear the sound he'd grown so accustomed to in the last few weeks hiding inside this deep voice. She explained that she automatically ran her voice through a pitch adjuster when she talked over the 'nets. She said she'd been living this way for so long that it wasn't until she was halfway across the world that she realized that she would probably look quite different to what she figured Dex imagined she looked like.

Her smile faltered and she took a large sip of her drink. Not looking Dex in the eye, she said, "So. Here I am. I don't really know what I'm doing here and I can go back anytime if this is inconvenient." Her eyes darted up to meet Dex's, then she looked away quickly again. "I shouldn't have come," she said quickly and made as if to stand up. "I'll just go." Dex reached out, touching her arm lightly. She made a noise and pulled her hand away, as if his touch had burned her.

"I'm sorry," Dex said, lightly, "but I don't want you to leave."

"No, I'm sorry," Annabelle said, her dark eyes shining above a light five o' clock shadow. "This might be a little too much for me... you know how I am about this," she waved her hands, gesturing at Dex's apartment, but meaning the whole physical world.

"I do," Dex said, looking up at her and smiling softly, "and you came anyway."

"I guess," she said, looking at him out the corner of her eye. She tentatively sat down. "I don't know if this is going to work," she said, sadly.

"Me neither," Dex said. "Who ever knows if anything is going to work? It doesn't really matter. What matters is that you came. You tried. I don't think anyone has ever tried that hard for me before."

"You're such a big sap," she said, laughing that laugh that Dex had grown to want to hear. He grinned and stood up.

"I've got an idea," he said, walking over to his comfortable chair. "You stay there and just follow my lead, okay?"

"Uh, sure," Annabelle sounded unconvinced, but she didn't move. Dex logged into Marionette City and pinged Annabelle with a link. "What are you doing?" she protested. "I'm right here."

"Just shut up and follow the link." He linked into the restaurant where they'd gone on that awful date and Annabelle appeared shortly thereafter.

"Oh," she said, a look of realization appearing on both her physical face and her avatar. Her avatar walked over to Dex, dressed in her usual business wear, which soon morphed into the shimmering fabric and bands outfit she'd had on for their abortive evening out. Dex quickly added his horrible date tie to his outfit and they were seated at a table. A bottle of wine appeared and Dex poured glasses for them both.

"This way neither of us are happy," he said aloud, causing Annabelle to shift focus briefly to Dex's apartment. She first looked shocked, then smiled, using both sets of lips.

"You are one funny guy, Andersson Dexter," she said, also aloud.

"I try," he said. They sat in silence for a while, Dex looking at the Annabelle who sat across his apartment, Annabelle looking at Dex's avatar.

"It won't be easy for me," Annabelle said, finally. "Every part of me wants to walk out your door and find somewhere to hide where no one can see me."

"It's bad for me, too," Dex said. "I hate having to meet you in this bubble," he waved his avatar's arms in Marionette City, "when I could just reach out..." Annabelle flinched and Dex and his avatar smiled. He had his avatar reach out across the table and touch Annabelle's hand. She took his hand in hers and smiled.

"It doesn't feel like anything to you, does it?" she asked, squeezing his hand.

"No, it feels like something," Dex said, sadly. "It feels like fraud, deception and insincerity." Annabelle let his hand go and looked down.

"We've got a long way to go, you and I," she said.

"Sure," Dex said. "We're all changing, all of us, all the time. People change and they grow apart. But, maybe sometimes it goes the other way, too."

# ACKNOWLEDGMENTS

This book went through many incarnations, and I owe many thanks to the members of my writing group who suffered though my early chapters: Kris Atwood, Linda Frear, Steven Ray Orr, Margaret Rolfe, and particularly Josh MacLeod, who first invented The Cubicle Men, albeit in a very different form.

I'm also deeply grateful to the many people who encouraged me after the release of *Beautiful Red*. Folks who stand out are Andrew Cornell, Steve Holden, Demian Petryshyn, Nobilis Reed and my mom, Shona Wehm.

I'm eternally thankful for all the notes by email, twitter, facebook comments and carrier pigeon from people who like my work. They are worth more than any publishing contract to me.

And as always, thanks to my first mate, Steven Ensslen, for everything.

# ABOUT THE AUTHOR

M. Darusha Wehm is a two-time Parsec Award finalist and author of the SF novels **Beautiful Red**, **Self Made**, **Act of Will** and **The Beauty of Our Weapons**.

Her short fiction has appeared in *Thaumatrope Magazine*, Podioracket's *Glimpses* anthology and *Luna Station Quarterly*.

In the physical world, she was a civil servant with the Government of Canada and is now engaged more or less full-time in writing.

She is based in Victoria, BC, Canada and is currently living in New Zealand after sailing down the west coast of the Americas and across the Pacific Ocean with her partner, Steven, on their sailboat, Scream.

For more information about her writing and her travels, visit Darusha on the web at http://darusha.ca.

www.ingramcontent.com/pod-product-compliance
Lightning Source LLC
Chambersburg PA
CBHW021042130626
46552CB00005B/1967